UNSPEAKABLE

ABBIE RUSHTON

UNSPEAKABLE

www.atombooks.net

ATOM

First published in Great Britain in 2015 by Atom

3 5 7 9 10 8 6 4

All characters and events in this publication, other than those clearly in the public domain, are fictitious and any resemblance to real persons, living or dead, is purely coincidental.

A CIP catalogue record for this book is available from the British Library.

ISBN 978-0-349-00206-4

Typeset in Palatino by M Rules
Printed and bound in Great Britain by
Clays Ltd, St Ives plc

Papers used by Atom are from well-managed forests and other responsible sources.

MIX
Paper from responsible sources
FSC® C104740

Atom
An imprint of
Little, Brown Book Group
100 Victoria Embankment
London EC4Y 0DY

An Hachette UK Company
www.hachette.co.uk

www.atombooks.net

For my grandparents, with love

CHAPTER ONE

The dog is drowning. His eyes are wide, bloodshot; his ears flattened against his head. I fling myself into the mud at the edge of the water and reach for him. *I won't let you die here.*

He tries to haul himself out, but his cream coat is saturated and the weight drags him back down. Labradors are supposed to be strong swimmers, but he looks like an old dog and is only just managing to keep afloat. His head sinks beneath the water. I count one breath. He doesn't emerge. Two. *Come on!* Three. He re-surfaces, water cascading off his face as he coughs and struggles to breathe.

Our eyes lock. The dog makes a weak, snuffling sound. Nothing like the loud barks that echoed through the woods a few minutes ago. He sounded so afraid, I left the footpath straight away, barging through brambles and bushes to find him.

I stretch out an arm, beckoning. The dog tries again. His paws dig deeper into the bank this time, his back legs kicking. I lean forward, cold sludge oozing beneath me, its fetid stench hitting the back of my throat. I can almost reach his nose, but there's nothing to grab hold of. A few more inches and I could latch on to his collar. But any further and I'll fall in myself. His whiskers tickle my skin and his hot breaths steam into my palm. I'm so close! My muscles are aching, screaming, shaking.

Just a bit further. You can do it!

But his claws rake through the mud and he sinks back with a whimper that makes my stomach clench. *No. Don't give up. Please!*

I rest back on my knees and cast a quick glance behind me. A blockade of trees conceals us from the main path. I listen, hoping I'll hear footsteps, but there's nothing. Just the murmur of wind rippling through leaves and the dog's clumsy paws smacking the water. Should I go and look for someone? I don't know what to do!

Then I hear a man's voice. Deep. Laced with worry. 'Jasper!' it calls. 'Jasper!'

The dog's head snaps up. He opens his mouth to bark, but swallows a mouthful of water instead.

The man sounds far away. I could try to find him, but I can't abandon Jasper.

Over here, I think. *We're over here.*

Thoughts are no good. I need words. They gather inside and claw up my throat like prisoners fighting to escape.

'Jasper! Jasper!' The man is afraid.

My words tumble over each other in their rush to break free.

The man's fear turns to anger. 'Jasper, come here *now*!'

I can do this!

A voice rips through my mind like a sharp, stabbing headache. I try not to listen, but it's so loud, so brutal, it just cuts through everything else.

No, you can't, Megan. You really can't.

And just like that, my words are gone.

A sound of raw frustration scrapes across my throat. I'm hopeless. Pathetic.

'Jasper!'

Driven by the sound of his owner's voice, Jasper prepares for one last push. In an instant I'm on my stomach again, leaning towards him. *Good boy! Clever dog.*

With a colossal effort, Jasper launches himself out of the water, at least halfway up the bank. I wrap my fingers around his collar, then I almost scream as my body lurches towards the water. For a few, slow-motion seconds, I'm dragged through the sludge, until my foot hooks on a rock. My shoulder jars and pain rips through my ankle, but we stop. I clench my teeth and heave. Jasper is wriggling and scrabbling. My grip loosens. No! I try to lock my fingers, but they're trembling too much. I'm going to lose him! I can't hold on!

Somehow, Jasper manages to propel himself up, knocking me backwards. The full weight of a sodden dog slams into my chest and forces the air from my lungs. I'm lying in the mud with a smelly, bedraggled dog on top of me. And I'm smiling, sucking in air, and crying at the same time.

Jasper rolls off me and shakes himself, peppering me with drops of dirty water. Then he flumps to the ground, panting. He looks at me and his tail twitches: a brave attempt at a wag. I stroke his ear and he nuzzles my palm, then licks my hand.

'Jasper!' The man staggers into the clearing, his voice husky. I lower my head and let my hair flop around my face.

'God, Jasper!' He kneels on the grass, running his hands over Jasper's damp fur. 'Are you OK?'

I'm not sure if he's talking to me or the dog. To be fair, neither of us is going to answer.

'What happened?'

I instruct my head to lift. Maybe I can smile at him? But my body is locked. I glimpse the man through my hair.

'Did he get stuck?'

I say nothing.

'I'm not going to hurt you.'

His tone is gentle, but it won't tempt my voice out.

'There's no need to be afraid.'

He doesn't seem surprised that I won't speak. It's almost like he understands. But that's stupid. Why would he?

'Can you tell me what happened?'

No.

'Didn't you hear me calling?'

Most people would be annoyed, but he just sounds curious. 'Are you all right?'

I want to answer him. He seems like a nice man. Yes, I think, coaxing the word as if it's a weak flame. But it fizzles out, leaving a sour, smoky taste on my tongue. Defeated, I nod.

The man sighs, but isn't ready to give up yet. 'Do you want me to call someone for you?'

I shake my head.

There's a light touch on my arm. I tense, but don't move away.

'I've got some towels in the back of my car. If you want to come with me, you could clean up a bit.'

Silence. I shake my head. *No.*

Thank you, I add.

'OK . . . I don't feel right about leaving you here, but I've got to get Jasper home.'

I peek out from under my hair. Jasper is shivering.

'It looks like you tried to help him. Thanks.'

I want to reply. I want to thank him for not trying to force me to speak, for not asking more questions, but he's already disappeared into the woods.

He must think I'm an idiot. The word ricochets around my mind. Idiot, idiot, idiot.

CHAPTER TWO

Twenty-one, twenty-two, twenty-three ... I'm standing by the door with my hand on the handle. The clock in the hallway ticks through the seconds ... twenty-six, twenty-seven, twenty-eight. Mum's heels clack down the stairs behind me. I get a waft of coconut conditioner. I don't need to turn to know the expression on her face is half bemused, half exasperated.

Thirty-four, thirty-five, thirty-six. When the clock reaches seven minutes and forty-eight seconds past eight, I haul down the handle and hurry out.

'Bye, Megan!' Mum calls after me.

I imagine saying goodbye, picture how Mum's brows would shoot up, how she'd smile and hug me, her eyes shiny with tears.

I lick my lips, open my mouth.

No!

My teeth snap shut. I wave instead. Mum waves back, then shivers and slams the door. The sun is shining, but it's spring and there's still a bite in the air. A beer can is picked up by the breeze and clatters across the street, stopping beside a pork scratchings packet that's been floating around for days.

I take quick steps, head down, hoping I won't see any of our neighbours. I've lived all of my fifteen years in Scrater's Close, and it is, without doubt, the biggest dump in the whole of the New Forest.

I don't want to be at the bus stop until twenty-one minutes past eight, so I dawdle a little in the village centre. There's not a lot going on in Brookby: one café, a couple of pubs, a Post Office, a tiny convenience store and a load of tacky tourist shops, full of spiritual stuff like crystals, incense, dragon models and wizard puppets.

There's a huddle of kids near the war memorial, most of them wearing identically hideous burgundy uniforms with the Barcham Green logo on. I glance up the road. No bus. Damn! I plod towards them, my stomach writhing.

It's the first day back after Easter and excitement crackles through the air as Lindsay and Grace gossip about Lindsay's ex, Josh takes the piss out of Callum's 'gay' trainers, and Sadie waves a flashy pink mobile around. 'My stepdad bought it for me,' she says, with a flick of her corn-coloured hair.

Something's going on. They're showing off more than usual. Everyone stands in a loose circle, jabbering and squawking like seagulls fighting over a chip. It can only mean one thing: a new person. I peer through the bodies and catch tantalising glimpses of black, corkscrew curls, a pair of peacock earrings, and skin the colour of frappuccino.

'I'm so jealous of your tan!'

'How come you're starting just before the exams?'

'Whose form are you going to be in? Do you want to sit next to me on the bus?'

If – by some miracle – Sadie isn't the one who gets her claws into the new girl, I try to figure out who she'll end up with. There's the fit-but-thick group, the boringly-average-in-every-way crowd, or – as a last resort – the weird-but-smart clique.

I don't slot into any of those. So I hover on the outskirts of the circle – a lone sparrow. At least they're distracted. At least they haven't noticed me yet.

The bus grumbles up beside the pavement. Sadie gets priority boarding. Everyone knows that, so we all hang back. Her Twiglet legs jerk beneath a tight skirt as she strides forward, a triumphant grin on her face, arm linked with the new girl. Sadie's new BFF has the honour of getting on first. I glance up and see two large, attractive eyes the shade of hazelnuts before she hurries up the steps.

Sadie puts her hand on the rail. Wow. She's actually going to leave me alone today! My muscles unclench, as if I've sunk into a hot bath. But I'm wrong. Of course I'm wrong. Sadie pauses – not caring that everyone is waiting for her – and looks over her shoulder at me. Her lips, slick with deep, red gloss, form one word: 'Freak.' She runs her tongue over her teeth, savouring it.

Lindsay gives me a look, daring me to fight back. I glare at the ground. I can think of a thousand things I'd like to say to Sadie, but all I do is blush and move to the back of the queue, wondering what happened to the girl I used to be friends with.

I know what Hana would've said: 'I'll tell you what's freaky – how Sadie's eyebrows are dark brown but she still claims to be a natural blonde.' I nod my head forward to hide my smile.

Sadie gets on the bus. As she struts to the back – the business class section – she looks down her nose at the plebs in the economy seats. She hates that she's not old enough to get a first-class seat on the last row, which is only for sixth-formers.

Lindsay follows, swinging her curved hips down the aisle, fingers twisting through her wispy brown hair. Half the boys on the bus turn to watch her go. She's wearing a white shirt with a lacy red bra beneath. Subtle.

Grace glides behind them, pale and willowy. She used to hate that skinny body, but now I think she loves being one of the thinnest girls in our year.

As soon as Sadie and her mates have got on, everyone surges forward. I wait at the back, eyes down, watching the scuffle of shoes. Callum's 'gay' trainers skirt to the front of the queue. Bad move. Someone snarls, 'Get to the back, queer-boy,' and gives him a shove. Callum stumbles, almost falls, but just about rights himself. He joins me at the back, calling them 'tossers' under his breath.

Poor Callum. I want to do something to show I understand,

but what? I reach back and squeeze his arm. A few seconds later, he whispers quietly, so only the two of us can hear, 'Thanks, Megan.'

I glance up at the bus. The new girl is staring out of the window, right at us. My eyes race back to the ground. I remind myself to exhale. I seem to have forgotten how this whole breathing thing works!

I'm the last to board the bus. Inside, the air is still and fusty: a nauseating concoction of cheesy feet, Red Bull and body odour. I feel like getting off again, until I see Luke smiling at me. He's in our usual seat near the front. He's been growing his sandy hair out and it falls around his ears, scruffy and tousled. I slip into the seat next to him, wishing I could return the smile.

'Hi, Megan. How's it going?' Luke asks.

I don't look up but manage a nod.

Luke starts to chat as if we're having a normal conversation. He's describing the orienteering he did last week. 'We were the other side of Lyndhurst. It's really nice out there.'

No it's not. It's dangerous.

I don't go to that side of the New Forest any more. Luke should know that, after what happened.

What happened because of you.

I stiffen. Luke carries on, oblivious. 'Can't believe it'll all be over after this term.'

I swallow heavily. Neither can I. I don't even want to think about that now.

Luke nudges me and grins. 'You think I should try for a seat on the back row in September?'

I shake my head. Luke should be up there in business class. He's clever, sporty, good-looking, but every day he sits here with me in the gum-spattered loser-seats. I wouldn't mind if he left. I know I'm not the best company. But we've been friends for a long time. We have this – I don't know – kind of bond, because of the things we know about each other. Things that will always stay just between us.

There's the rustle of a crisp packet behind me. It's Simon, Luke's brother. 'Hi, Megan.' He leans further over the seat and gusts of cheese and onion breath billow into my face. 'Did you see that programme? About the army?'

I look down and shake my head, but he starts to gush about it anyway. Simon speaks in short bursts, like machine gun fire: bom-bom-bom-bom. 'It was awesome! They had this one bloke, lost half his face. IED explosion.'

Luke has turned away to look out of the window, a wry smile on his lips. Simon prattles on, glad to talk to someone who won't tell him to shut up. He's halfway through a monologue about facial disfigurements when a ball of paper soars past his ear and lands in Luke's lap. It unfurls a little and we catch a glimpse of handwriting. Skin grafts and missing limbs forgotten, Simon cranes his head to try to see what it says.

Luke flicks it to the floor without opening it, his jaw tight with anger. Simon stares for a moment, then sits back to continue his crisp crunching. Luke and I settle into silence, but we both keep looking at that ball of paper.

In the end, I sigh and lean forward to get it.

Luke grabs my hand. 'Don't.'

But I can't just leave it. I shake him off and pick it up, opening it discreetly on my lap: *What noise does a mute girl make when you ...*

I screw the paper into a ball as if I could crush the words, but not before Luke has seen. He swears, then turns to glare at the road. The back of his neck is red.

I fumble in my bag and tear a corner off my homework planner. *Ignore them,* I scribble. The corners of Luke's mouth twist into a sad smile.

I wish I had the guts to turn back and glare at the morons who wrote it. Is it so unbelievable that Luke and I are just friends? I don't fancy him. And he definitely doesn't fancy me. When Hana was still around, he only had eyes for her.

The bus continues out of Brookby, and within moments we're surrounded by open, expansive heathland. It's smattered with splashes of vivid yellow gorse against the green bracken.

A herd of wild ponies zigzags across the heath. Their manes whip through the wind and their hooves carve out clods of earth that fly up behind them. A couple of them make a sudden swerve on to the road. Our driver stamps on the brake and we all jerk forward. Simon thumps into the back of my seat and a girl behind us lets out a little shriek.

There's a pony right next to the window. Its rust-coloured coat is flecked with sweat and I can see every beautiful curve of its muscles. The herd moves on, away from the road. They're so erratic, exhilarating. I don't tear my gaze away until they've cantered and frolicked into the distance.

There's a new English teacher at school: Mrs Austin. Her head wobbles on top of a long neck like a nodding Churchill dog. A secret smile sneaks across my face as I imagine her saying, 'Oh, yes' in a deep Leeds accent.

Mrs Austin asks, 'What makes Caliban's speech so compelling in this scene?'

No one responds. Undaunted by the steely silence, Austin's eyes roam the room. They rest on me. Heat rises from my toes and devours my neck, ears, face.

Please don't ask me.

But she asks my name, then glances at the register.

Just leave me alone.

I shake my head. I tilt it forward so my hair falls in two curtains around my face. I have an answer, but the words are locked deep within me and I can't summon them to the surface. My classmates' stares bore tiny holes into me. I clench my hands.

Finally, someone breaks the agonising silence. 'She doesn't speak, Miss.' Sadie's voice is saturated with smugness.

There's an awkward pause. Someone must've told her about me, surely? Mrs Austin nods, gives an answer herself and moves on quickly.

As we file out of the classroom, Sadie flounces up with Lindsay and Grace at her heels, practically salivating on her legs. Sadie makes a big deal of saying, 'You're welcome.' Grace titters obligingly.

My eyes flee to the ground and my arms wrap around my waist, but inside I'm seething. *You cow. I still have a voice, even if I can't use it. One day, when I can speak again, I'll tell you exactly what I think of you.*

Sadie sticks her nose in the air and leaves.

I sigh. *One day, when I can speak again* ... Yeah, like that's going to happen. Like I'd risk revealing the truth. No. I'll stay quiet. After all, there's no one better than a mute to keep a secret.

CHAPTER THREE

When the bus chucks us out in Brookby after school, there are a few sightseers still milling around, clutching bags of sticky fudge. A pony and trap rattles along the road, carrying a couple of Asian tourists who huddle together against the cold, smiles frozen to their faces.

As I pass the café, I peer through the steamy windows to see if Mum's still there. She's wiping down a table with brisk, impatient swipes. I bet she's craving a cigarette – she has that slightly ratty look on her face.

I can't get used to seeing Mum with her hair tied back. She hates it, but her boss makes her. 'Man's a health and safety Nazi,' she says. 'Should've seen his face when he found a fake nail in the egg mayonnaise. Had the nerve to accuse me! I mean, it was Electric Cherry, for God's sake, Megan. Who does he think I am?'

Mum brushes a few loose strands of hair from her face. Her roots are starting to show. They're dark blonde, in contrast to the yellowy colour she dyes it. I must get my brown, wavy mop from Dad, although I've never seen a photo of him.

Mum straightens, spots me and waves. I wave back, then turn away and carry on home.

A row of trees lines the main road. I look up, listening for birdcalls and chirps, the rustle and whisper of wind darting through leaves. The branches form a canopy above me, like parents holding umbrellas over their children. The trees have been here all my life, as ancient and sturdy as Grandpa, though they have survived him by three years.

Mr Wexford dodders along the pavement towards me, shuffling and sniffing like a hedgehog. Back stooped, flat cap perched on his head, a walking stick in his trembling hand, he's the picture of a frail, kindly old man. But I know better.

Mr Wexford – like many locals – doesn't approve of Scrater's Close. Brookby is full of thatched cottages and converted barns, gardens that brim with roses, lavender, honeysuckle. Scrater's is two long terraces of scruffy houses with rubbish-tip gardens, graffitied garages, and several obnoxious residents.

As I pass him, Mr Wexford's moustache twitches. It's tinged pink where he's spilled his medicine. It would be sweet if he weren't such a horrible old git. 'Bloody scallywags,' he spits.

I try to muster a scathing retort.

Don't be stupid.

I bite back a gasp. As he passes, Mr Wexford glowers at me. Then, with a whiff of TCP, he's gone.

I stomp down Scrater's, glaring at the dirt-coloured garages and the burnt-out husk of a car outside Number 5. Why the hell don't they move it? Or mow their lawn, for that matter?

Mr Wexford is right. Scrater's clings to the edge of Brookby like a slug on an orchid. A lot of villagers wish that the whole street could be scooped up and dumped in some grotty city. Then Brookby would actually be in with a chance of winning that stupid 'Village of the Year' award they're all so obsessed with.

Do they think we chose to live here? Did they imagine that people looked around loads of houses, weighed up their options and said, 'Yes, I'll take the one with the back door that's been kicked in and the neighbours who chuck cigarette stubs over the fence, just next to the phone box that's been smashed to pieces'? Idiots.

As soon as I get home, I prise off my shoes and peel the socks from my feet. I set the shoes in their correct place on the floor, aligning them at a right angle to the scuff mark on the wall.

I head to the kitchen in search of food, but the fridge offers nothing more than a sour, gone-off-milk smell and a couple of shrivelled carrots, and the only thing in the cupboards is a packet of dried cheese sauce that's three months out of date.

Last night's washing up festers in the sink, the plates encrusted with dried tomato sauce. *Double rank*, Hana would say. She never made me feel embarrassed, though. She'd just laugh, grab a sponge, and help me to clean up.

I can't cope with this. I have to sort it out now. I let the water run until it's steaming, then squirt a load of washing-up liquid in the bowl. I reach for the rubber gloves, then pause, a gentle smile on my face. Gran taught me to always wear rubber gloves. She said you could tell a lot about someone from their hands. Hers were wrinkled and gnarled with arthritis, but they were so, so soft. She'd taken care of them all her life. I loved the way her skin folded around her wedding ring, as if it had become a natural part of her body.

I practically grew up at Gran and Grandpa's. They looked after me while Mum was at work. They did everything they could to fill the gap left by Dad, who buggered off three months after Mum found out she was pregnant. They didn't speak to him after that. They were ashamed to call him their son.

I close my eyes. I can almost smell the sweet scent of Grandpa's baking brownies. In an instant, I'm back in their house, sitting at the kitchen table. Grandpa's wearing a pink, floral apron. I know he's done it just to make me laugh. It never fails.

'Here you go, chicken,' he says, setting a hot tray down in front of me and ruffling my hair. 'Don't burn yourself.'

I grab a spoon, poking it through the crust to the wonderfully gooey bit beneath.

I blink and I'm back in our own miserable kitchen, staring at the pile of dirty dishes. I leave them to soak. I align all the mugs in the cupboard so the handles face right, then I tidy up the sprawling mess of Mum's bills and letters. I sit on the sofa and run my fingers through the tassel on the cushion, then I trace the familiar whirls and flounces of the pattern on the fabric.

I need to get out.

I rush upstairs to change. Then I open my top drawer and pull out Grandpa's camera. It's in a special, velvet-lined case. A Canon EOS 5 with a 100–300mm zoom lens. It's one of the old ones you put film in. Grandpa didn't upgrade to digital. He said his favourite part of photography was the suspense, the uncertainty, as he waited for his 'snaps' to be developed.

I leap down the stairs and get my old bike from the utility room. Outside, I pedal furiously until I reach the cattle grid at the top of the street, where I gently bump over the ridges. On the other side, I charge down the main road, my feet whizzing as I swerve past a couple of donkeys.

I see Mum before she sees me. She clicks down the pavement in a pair of ruby heels, an unlit cigarette dangling from her mouth, which gleams with coral lipstick. When she looks up, she whips the cigarette out and tries to hide it behind her back.

I coast to a stop next to her. Mum's hair looks limp, and her make-up is just a thin covering for the tiredness around her eyes. I pretend not to notice her guilty expression.

'Hello, you.' She gives me a weary sigh. I wonder if I should change my plans and go home with her. She looks knackered. 'You off out again?'

I shrug and point in the direction of home, as if to say: 'I don't have to.'

She doesn't get it, though. 'You don't know if you're going out? You might be going that way?'

I shrug again.

Mum rustles a carrier bag. 'I've got some bits here. I don't think we have much else in.' She frowns, as if she's disappointed. It'll be leftovers from the café: hard baguettes stuffed with sweaty cheese and wilting salad, or a couple of stale slices of lemon cake. I want to tell her it's all right, I don't care that it's not proper food, but we both know that Grandpa would disapprove.

'Well, I'll see you at home then.'

One of Mum's hands is still behind her back. I point at it and raise my brows.

'What?' she says, widening her eyes in fake innocence.

I make a grab for her arm, just as she's about to flick the cigarette into some bushes behind her. She laughs and tries to twist away from me. 'OK, OK! You caught me.'

She waves the cigarette in my face. I giggle and try to snatch it from her, but she's too fast. 'Just one, Megan,' she pleads. 'I need one today. Some silly tart thought she saw mould on one of the sandwiches. I tried to tell her it was just a bit of flour, but she went off on one. Made a right scene.'

I smile, then push off from the pavement.

'Be back before dark!' she yells as I fly downhill.

I stop at the village green, where a small herd of cows has gathered. There's a ripple of twitching tails and waggling ears as they try to dislodge flies. I take out Grandpa's camera and frame a shot of a frisky new calf with its mother, a grand beech tree sweeping into the sky above them.

Soon I'm pedalling along a road that cuts across the heath. I feel like I've barely been able to breathe until now. I gulp in lungfuls of air. I'm moving so fast the wind whips tears from my eyes and nips at my knuckles.

I leave my bike in a car park off the main road, then set off down a trail. As I walk, I reach out to touch everything. I want to feel it all: the bristle of a gorse bush, the gentle tickle of leafy bracken, the scratch of tree bark. My limbs loosen and lengthen, my shoulders drop, and my heart rate slows.

Twenty minutes later, I reach a small patch of woodland. A stream darts between the trees, filling the forest with its gentle laughter, and a squirrel spirals down a tree trunk like it's a helter-skelter. I take a photo of the waning sun shooting spears of light through the leaves.

I settle on a bridge, place the camera down and swing my feet over the edge. I reach into my pocket and draw out a notebook and a pen. After sucking on the lid for a few seconds, I begin to write.

CHAPTER FOUR

Dear Hana,

Today was the first day back at school. It was pretty rubbish. Sadie's being an über-bitch at the moment. If there were an Olympic sport in bitchery, she'd be a champion. I wish I could've told her so. I know you wouldn't have taken any crap from her.

Jayne's got this new haircut that makes her look like Prince Harry. I swear, if you could see it, you'd laugh your head off.

What else? We've got a supply teacher for Maths. I can't remember her name but she has rancid breath and you can see her leg hairs poking through her tights. It's gross, but still more interesting than quadratic equations.

The first tourists arrived a few weeks ago. They were wearing shorts. Shorts! Even though it was frigging freezing. They had bumbags and stupid caps on, and were taking pictures of everything. You'd think they'd never seen a post box before.

I should go now. Mum will be stressing if I'm not back soon.

I'm sorry about what happened. If I could change it all, I would.

I miss you.

Megan xxx

CHAPTER FIVE

Halfway through a spectacularly dull PSHE lesson about Internet safety, I raise my hand and show my permission slip. A quick nod from the teacher and I leave, making my way to the stationery cupboard where I have my sessions with Ms Cole, the psychologist who visits once a week. I imagine she'll be shuffling her battered deck of cards, ready for me to beat her at rummy again.

The door is usually ajar, but it's closed today, so I knock and wait. It opens. But the person inside isn't Ms Cole. I can't quite believe who it is. Clearly, the feeling's mutual, as there are a good ten seconds of silence before he manages to speak. 'Ah, Megan. This, er … explains a lot. Come in, come in,' says the nice man with a dog called Jasper.

I stay put.

'Oh, sorry,' he adds. 'I'm Mr Harwell. Ms Cole's replacement. Didn't you receive the letter that was sent home?'

Evidently not.

Mr Harwell takes a deep breath, pushing it out through his teeth. 'I thought it would've been explained to you. I'll be taking your sessions from now on.'

I don't move.

'I hope that's OK?'

I liked Ms Cole. Why did she have to leave?

'Um, look. I didn't mean to spring this on you. If you just want to come and sit quietly with me, that's fine. In fact, it would give me a chance to catch up on some notes!'

I risk a quick look. Mr Harwell smiles. It's a good, genuine smile. I step into the stationery cupboard. A broken photocopier lurks in the corner, draped with dust and cobwebs. The bowing shelves are mounded with boxes, some battered and shabby, others new and almost overflowing with precious supplies of biros and pencils. There's barely space for the tiny coffee table and chairs that have been crammed in. I sit in my usual seat and start to pick at a hole in the material, digging my finger into the springy foam padding.

While he's faffing around with paperwork, I sneak another glance at Mr Harwell. He's clean-shaven, though there's an overlooked patch of stubble near his wiry, brown sideburns. His eyes are grey and serious, almost too old for the rest of his face. I'd guess he's in his early thirties.

When Mr Harwell pulls a pen out of his pocket and turns to a new page in his notebook, my gaze flicks back to the floor. What happens now? My breaths become shallow and laboured. Sweat dampens my palms.

'You'll be pleased to know that Jasper's doing fine,' he says.

Before I can stop myself, I look up and offer a small smile.

Mr Harwell nods, but doesn't write anything down. 'Well, thank you once again for coming to the rescue.'

He leans back in his chair and crosses one leg over his knee, like a psychologist in a film. He'd just need to steeple his fingers and rest his chin on them to complete the cliché. 'I understand you're quite the expert at rummy?'

I should be, the amount of practice I used to get.

'Rummy aside, is there anything you particularly enjoyed about your sessions with Ms Cole? Anything you'd like us to continue?'

I shrug.

'Her records say that you were sometimes able to write to her. There's no pressure, but if you'd like to write me a note, you're always welcome to.'

I nod, but make no move towards the blank writing pad he's left open on the table.

'I'm afraid we won't be playing cards today, Megan.'

I glance up, suspicious. This wasn't how Ms Cole worked. I liked our silent card games. Never mind the fact that, in seven months, I never said an entire word. Why does he want to change everything?

Wait! What if he changes *me*? What if he tricks me into talking? What if he finds out?

He can't EVER find out.

No. I can't! I need to leave!

I start to get up, just as Mr Harwell says, 'I'd like to try some breathing techniques.'

I stop by the door.

'It's OK, Megan. There's no need to feel self-conscious. We can do them together.'

Just breathing techniques? Nothing more?

'If you sit down again, I'll show you.'

I take a few unsteady steps back to my chair.

'We're going to start off by taking a nice, deep breath in through our noses, and back out through our mouths. Can you do that with me?'

Mr Harwell has a stray nostril hair that wiggles every time he exhales. He must mistake my smile as a sign that I'm going to join in, because he nods encouragingly. Guess I don't have much choice now. I lower my eyes and start to match my breaths with his. Slowly in, and slowly out again.

'Good! Now, what I want you to do, Megan, is start to feel your ribs moving in and out, so it's a really deep breath. If you put your hands on your stomach, you shouldn't feel it move at all.'

I try this. For a few moments we fill the room with the sound of our breathing. Mr Harwell's breath smells of strawberry yoghurt. I suddenly fancy a Fruit Corner. Hana's mum used to give them to us as a post-school snack on Mondays, Tuesdays and Thursdays. Wednesdays and Fridays were 'treat' days, when we'd get to choose a chocolate bar from the old cream-cracker tin.

I'm just starting to feel like a balloon that will burst if I take any more air in, when Mr Harwell announces that we've done enough. Really? That's it? I just have to sit here and breathe? Maybe this won't be so bad after all.

But then he says, 'Next week we'll try some other relaxation techniques.'

He can try. You still won't talk.

I wince. Mr Harwell doesn't notice – he's scrawling something on his notepad. 'If you've got any questions in the meantime,' he says, tearing the page out, 'here's my email address.'

I stare at it for a moment. Ms Cole never gave me her email address. I fold it neatly into four, say *thank you* in my head, and leave.

Luke's got basketball tonight so he won't be catching the bus. I still sit in the aisle seat because it's my seat. It wouldn't feel right to sit in the window seat.

I watch everyone file on. Lindsay has tied her shirt in a knot above her belly button. The bra is turquoise today, even though everyone knows that the head, Mr Finnigan, has had words.

Josh, who is sporting a black eye from a football match, barges past Callum, grunting, 'Out of the way, gay-boy.' He's about twice the size of Callum, who silently steps aside, a slight flush to his cheeks. My stomach squeezes. I almost shift across so he can sit next to me, but he quickly finds somewhere else.

Sadie and the new girl are amongst the last to get on. A kid loiters in the aisle, chatting to his friend about some collectible card he wants to swap. He's oblivious to the fact he's in Queen Sadie's way. She huffs, then snaps, 'For God's sake!' and shoves him in the back. The kid lurches forward and ends up sprawled across his friend's lap with his feet poking comically off the end of the seat.

The new girl's jaw drops. She's standing behind Sadie and shoots her a disgusted look. Then she glances round. Unusually for me, I'm slow off the mark and she catches my eye, throwing me a look that says, 'Can you believe she just did that?'

I freeze, floundering in her gaze. I wish I could raise my eyes as if to say, *That's nothing. That's tame for her.*

Don't you dare!

I whip back and stare at the seat in front, heart pulsing a wild beat.

Further towards the back of the bus, Sadie is yelling at one of the boringly average girls. 'Move, Smelly Ellie. Jasmine doesn't want to share a seat with you. You might contaminate her.'

Jasmine. The new girl's name. Grandpa used to grow jasmine. I close my eyes and can almost smell it drifting through the bus door. I imagine him pottering in his garden on a summer afternoon, coming in late to dinner and being gently nagged by Gran about his dirty hands. I remember those hands so clearly: the tiny crescents of soil nestled beneath his nails, the lines of dirt that wound through the creases of his palms.

My eyes snap open when I realise Jasmine is talking. Her voice is deep and smooth as honey, the edges of her words neat and rounded. Her English is good, but by the way she pronounces some things, I'd guess she wasn't brought up in the UK, or that she speaks more than one language. 'It's fine, Sadie, really,' she's saying. 'I'll just sit somewhere else.'

'No, you won't,' Sadie snaps, unwilling to relinquish her prize. 'Move your fat arse, Ellie.'

Ellie scowls and mutters something about being there first, but gathers her things and starts to shift.

Jasmine casts an apologetic look in Ellie's direction. 'It's honestly fine.'

Sadie's eyes bulge as she hisses, 'If you want to hang around with us, you need to sit with us. Got it?'

Jasmine's response is amazing. Just stunning. Without blinking, she says, 'Got it,' and turns away from Sadie to look for another seat.

If this were a film, there would be a collective gasp of horror. No one treats Sadie like that. For a few seconds, Sadie can't seem to find the words. How satisfying. She stares at Jasmine in disbelief, then her eyes narrow until they're nothing but two seething slits.

'Fine,' she yells. 'Go and sit where you belong: with the rest of the losers.' Her tone is scathing, but even the heavy layer of make-up can't conceal the blush spreading over her skin. Sadie's embarrassed. And she'll make Jasmine pay for that.

CHAPTER SIX

'Scooch over, will you?' Jasmine says as she stands beside my seat. I jump. I actually jump. How embarrassing. I fumble with my bag and coat, then shuffle across to the window seat. Jasmine drops down beside me. I get a waft of something sweet and smoky – incense, perhaps.

'I'm supposed to be keeping my head down and not getting into trouble, but she's definitely trouble, right? What a nutter!'

Damn right, I reply in my head. But my mouth says nothing.

This doesn't seem to bother Jasmine, who launches into a blow-by-blow account of her first day. Barely stopping to breathe, she tells me how she almost ended up in the boys' changing room when she was looking for the IT suite ('I was lost – honest!'), that she made her whole History class crack up when she accidentally called Ms Dilby 'Sir' (an easy mistake to make), and how the vegetarian lasagne here is much better than the 'minging' stuff they served at her old school.

As Jasmine talks, I stare out of the window. I know it's rude. I hate it. I just can't help it. She must think I'm bored. But I'm not – I'm captivated. Clinging to each of her words like they're monkey bars and I'm leaping from one to the next, terrified that she'll just stop and leave me dangling. There's a brief pause, and I hold my breath, but Jasmine just takes a sip of water and continues.

'My mum's Cypriot but my dad's English so I grew up over there but we moved to Portsmouth last summer because Dad lost his job. Isn't the New Forest ace? Mum and I went for a walk at the weekend and it's gorgeous. Anyway, Mum's got this admin job in a solicitor's in Ringwood. She says it's really dull, but we need the money because Dad hasn't had a permanent job in, like, eight months. He used to be a sales manager in Cyprus but he's really struggled to find anything out here.'

There's a two-second silence, then: 'You don't talk much, do you?'

My eyes remain locked on the hedgerow whizzing past outside. I shake my head.

'I mean, I know I talk *a lot* but you don't seem to talk *at all*.'

I fight to swallow the lump in my throat, try to stop my nails from piercing the soft skin of my palm. I nod, bracing myself for the inevitable. She'll either find an excuse to move seats, or ask one of the usual stupid questions, like: 'Why don't you speak?', 'Can you just say one word to me?', or, my personal favourite, 'If you had to speak or eat puke, which would you do?'

But Jasmine just smiles and carries on. 'My sister Lily started at the primary school today. I hope she's been OK. She's quite shy. Yeah, I know what you're thinking: Jasmine and Lily. My mum has a thing for flowers. Well, you'd be kind of right. She has more of a thing for smells. It sounds strange, but you'll know what I mean when you come round. You will come round some time this week, won't you?'

What? She doesn't even know me!

Jasmine spots my surprise and her face drops. 'Sorry. I'm being too full-on. I do that.' There's a pause. Jasmine nibbles on her lower lip. Then she suddenly says, 'It's just ... the thing is ... I think it's cool that you don't hang around with Sadie the sadist. What's your name?'

I stare at her helplessly. My name. I can't even answer a simple question!

Jasmine doesn't wait for me to find something to write on, but leans over the back of our seat. 'Hey,' she calls out, 'what's this girl's name?'

I blush and wriggle down, willing my body to liquefy into a puddle on the floor. A head pops up behind me.

Niall Lewis grunts, 'I dunno.'

He doesn't know? He's been sitting on the same bus as me for years! Am I invisible?

His mate, Andy, pipes up with, 'That's Megan Thomas. She's the one who doesn't speak.'

Jasmine twists to face me. 'Nice to meet you, Megan-who-doesn't-speak.' She grabs my hand and gives it a firm, business-like shake. Her skin is soft and smooth and cool.

Andy's head pops round the side of our seat. 'How come you moved schools just before exams?' he asks Jasmine. 'You get excluded from your last place?'

Jasmine looks away. 'No, I just . . . Well, I . . . It doesn't matter.'

Andy gives her a long look and is about to say something else when Niall distracts him with a video on his phone of a camel farting. As Jasmine looks at me, I quickly wipe any trace of curiosity from my face. There must be a reason for her changing schools just before GCSEs, but she obviously doesn't want to talk about it.

Jasmine begins to describe the weird stuff they found in the loft when they moved in. I shoot little glances at her. She's curvy without being overweight, pretty without being knockout gorgeous. Her eyes are wide and she has very dark lashes. Delicate laughter lines frame her lips.

Jasmine easily fills the rest of the journey with chatter. By the time the bus stops at Brookby, I'm breathless, dizzy, and completely dazzled.

Jasmine lives in Willingham Road. Scrater's is on the way so we walk home together, her voice burbling and gushing like a river. She sometimes slows down or speeds up, stumbles over things, changes course. I'm just happy to be caught up in it all, bobbing along with her, trying to keep my head above the current.

We turn a corner and almost collide with someone on a bike. Owen Morris – seventeen, recently in trouble with the police, and my next-door neighbour – swears, executes a quick turn, and eyes us angrily. 'Watch it!' he says.

But his expression changes when he notices Jasmine. He gives her a sleazy smile. 'Haven't seen you before. You new?'

'Yes,' Jasmine replies.

We carry on walking. Uninvited, Owen rides beside us. His blond hair is gelled into neat little spikes and he has these intense blue eyes that are so clear you'd never think he'd do anything wrong. He's ripped, too. I can see the shape of a six-pack through his tight T-shirt, which stretches over his sculpted upper arms. Half the girls in the village fancy him. Owen doesn't do much for me, but then he is one of Sadie's cast-offs.

'Where you from?' he asks Jasmine.

'Cyprus, originally. We moved to England last summer.'

He thinks for a moment. 'Cyprus. Is that like Greece?'

Jasmine smiles. I can tell he's blown away by her. 'Sort of. It's not far from Greece.'

Another boy whistles past on a battered bike, his shirt billowing in the wind.

Owen's face darkens. 'Oi!' he bellows. 'You owe me a tenner!'

The other boy slows, but doesn't stop. 'What for?'

'Them fags I bought you the other day.'

The boy is almost at the end of the road now. 'You smoked half of 'em!'

'All right, you owe me a fiver then.'

But the boy is already gone. Owen snorts and crams a cigarette in his mouth, never taking his eyes from Jasmine. 'What's your name?'

'Jasmine,' she replies with a shy smile, her cheeks glowing.

I shoot her a horrified look. Please don't tell me she's fallen for the bad boy thing!

'See you around, Jasmine.'

I hate the way he says her name, like he's tasting it.

Owen takes off, making sure he leaves an impression by doing a wheelie. Jasmine says, 'Well, that was . . . interesting.' I can hear the smile in her voice.

Please don't go there, Jasmine. Don't give Sadie another reason to hate you.

We carry on down Scrater's. Jasmine starts to describe an argument she had with her mum over school shoes, but I have to cut her short when we reach my house.

There's an awkward silence. I bet she can't wait to get away. She's just talked at me for over half an hour and I haven't responded once.

Because you have nothing to say!

'I'm sorry,' Jasmine mumbles. 'I know I've been rabbiting on. I just really want to make new friends. You've probably been thinking, For God's sake, shut up!'

No. Please don't ever shut up.

Jasmine scuffs her shoe against a weed poking out of a cracked pavement slab. 'Shall I call for you tomorrow? If you don't want me to, you can let me know. I mean, you can be honest if you just want me to get lost.'

My eyes widen. I wish Jasmine could see them, but my head is lowered. *Is she joking? Is she really asking to be my friend?*

Who'd want to be your friend?

I flinch, then shake my head to unstick the words. Jasmine thinks I'm saying no. 'OK. That's fine. I guess I'll see you around.' Her voice is so sad. She's turning to leave.

Don't let her go, idiot! Stop her! I reach out and tap Jasmine on the arm. She looks back and I try to meet her eyes. I get as far as her mouth before my nerve fails. When I nod, her lips curve into a hesitant smile. 'Is that a yes? You want me to call for you tomorrow?'

Another nod. She can't see, but I'm smiling too: a proper, wide smile. It's been so long, the muscles in my jaw seem to yawn and stretch.

'Cool. Great. See you tomorrow!'

I'll see you tomorrow. Wow. I really will see you tomorrow!

By the next morning, I've convinced myself that she's not going to come. Why would she? Why would someone like her want to spend time with me? She was just being polite. It was sweet of her, but that's all it was.

I'm halfway through a bowl of cereal when the doorbell rings. Seconds later, the letter box flies open and a voice dances into my house. 'Hello?' it calls. 'Megan? I didn't know what time you left so I stopped by early. Hello?'

Oh my God. My spoon drops, clattering against the side of the bowl. She's here! She's really here! My grin is so wide it almost splits my face in two.

I scramble around, grabbing the sandwiches I've just made

and ramming them into my bag. I scoop a pile of books from the table and throw them in, probably squashing the sandwiches.

The bathroom door creaks open and Mum's footsteps tip-tap across the landing. If she finds out Jasmine's here, she'll get all excited and want to meet her. I can't bear the embarrassment. I sprint out of the kitchen and down the hallway. I open the door just in time to see Jasmine's retreating back.

She turns and smiles. 'Oh, hi. Sorry, I know I'm early. What time do you normally leave?'

I can't answer that. *'Yes' or 'no' questions only, please*. I expect her to be mortified by her mistake, but Jasmine just laughs. 'God, Megan. I completely forgot. Duh! You ready? Shall we make a move?'

My eyes flit to the clock. Fifty-six minutes and eleven seconds past seven – way too early. I hover in the doorway. Jasmine tilts her head, puzzled. She must think I'm deranged, just standing here like this.

'Megan?' Mum yells from the top of the stairs. 'Is someone there? Thought I heard the bell.'

That's enough to propel me across the threshold, slamming the door behind me.

As we walk, I run my fingers along the splintery slats of our fence, slowing my breathing as I concentrate on their familiar shape.

Not long after we've passed the Morris residence, someone opens an upstairs window and wolf-whistles. Jasmine spins round, blushing and giggling. Something falls from her pocket:

a piece of lined notepaper with her name on it. I touch her arm and hand it back. Jasmine's smile evaporates. 'Thanks,' she says, crumpling it up and muttering something about moving here to get away from all this crap.

I frown, but don't push any further. I couldn't, even if I wanted to. It's not like I can just open my mouth and ask her.

You'll say nothing.

'Oh, I didn't tell you, Mum's going to enrol me on a Drama course over the summer. How cool is that? I'll be performing in the West End before you know it! I can't wait to go to the theatre. There aren't many in Cyprus. There's no West End. But there's nothing like the West End anywhere. I suppose there's Broadway in New York. One day I'm going to go there.'

She stops suddenly, right next to a cut-through we call Dog Poo Alley. 'Is this a short cut to the bus stop?'

I pause for a moment, before nodding. I never go down there. It's disgusting.

'C'mon then. We might as well.'

I don't move.

Jasmine smiles and grabs my hand. I stare for a moment, mesmerised by the way her tanned fingers interweave with mine, so pale in comparison. She does it as if it's the most natural thing in the world, as if we've been friends for years. I don't want her to let go, so I follow.

About halfway down the alley, Jasmine stops. Someone has crudely sprayed the words, 'JASMIN IS WELL FIT' across the fence. Like the dogs who mark their territory along the alley, Owen Morris is telling others that Jasmine is his.

Jasmine is silent for a moment, then she says, 'I actually think that's pretty cool.'

I don't. It's creepy.

How can I warn her away from Owen? If it hadn't been for him and his stupid ... A memory almost surfaces, but I push it down. Not now. I can't think about that now, or I'll lose it in front of Jasmine. And that can never happen.

Sadie's waiting for us at the bus stop. 'You,' she jabs a manicured finger at Jasmine, 'have made a very bad choice.' She looks me up and down. 'Her? Seriously?'

Jasmine's about to reply when the bus thunders up. We stand back to let everyone pass.

'What a bitch!' Jasmine's arms are locked by her sides, hands clenched so tightly her fingers are going red. 'Who does she think she is, talking about you like that? I'm going to ...' She closes her eyes, takes a deep breath. 'I'm going to do absolutely nothing,' she says quietly, almost to herself, 'because I need to focus on my exams.'

Luke is looking out for me on the bus with a hopeful expression on his face. I give him an apologetic wave and point to Jasmine's back. His smile fades, though he shrugs, as if it's all fine.

I slip into the seat next to Jasmine, feeling a bit unnerved about the new location two rows closer to the back. She shoots me an approving look. 'He's nice-looking.'

Is he?

'Yeah. Come on, Megan, you can't tell me you haven't noticed!'

Why haven't I noticed?

'Do you want to go and sit with him? I don't mind.'

I shake my head.

'He looked gutted when you walked past. I don't want to steal you away.'

I shake my head again.

Jasmine springs out of her chair. 'Let's go and sit over there.' She points to the seat across the aisle from Luke. 'I want to ask him about some revision.'

I give her a grateful smile and we move. Jasmine leans across and taps Luke on the shoulder. 'Hi, I'm Jasmine. You're in my History class, aren't you?'

'Yeah.'

'Can you give me a hand with something? We didn't really cover it at my old school.'

Luke isn't particularly talkative, though of course that doesn't put Jasmine off, and they start to chat. I tune out, looking through the window.

That night, I lie in bed, staring at the ceiling. I can't stop wondering if Jasmine would be better off making friends with someone else. I'm just not good for people. I ruin things. And Jasmine, she's special. I don't want to hurt her.

How can I explain? Maybe I could write an anonymous note

to warn her away from me? Would that work? It wouldn't work with Luke. He knows the worst there is to know about me, and he stuck around.

I text Hana:

Am I a bad friend?

I grip the phone, stare at the blank screen, willing it to light up. Come on, Hana. But there's nothing. No reply. What did I expect?

I hurl my phone against the wall. I suddenly feel like throwing a whole lot more. I grab my bedside lamp, almost yank it out of the wall, then force myself to stop and put it down again. I twist the duvet between my hands, tighter and tighter, until my arms start to shake, then I release it and drop back on to the pillow, panting.

I take a couple of Mr Harwell's deep breaths, then fall into an uneasy sleep. I'm swinging across a great, dark void, but something's wrong. I feel unsafe, afraid. I don't know what's beneath me, but I don't like it. Then I'm somewhere else, and Jasmine is there. I'm hurting her. Physically hurting her. I don't know how, but I can't stop. I hate it. Hate myself. My head fills with her screams.

My eyes snap open.

That last scream was real.

My heart stutters, then starts to hammer, sending pulses of fear through my body. I stumble into the corridor. Moments later, Mum joins me, her face pale without make-up, her eyes groggy and half closed.

'What's going on?' she rasps.

My brain hasn't quite woken up yet, and I actually open my mouth to say, 'I don't know.'

Don't even think about it.

The words dry up. I shake my head. We hear an almighty crash, followed by a roar of vicious, raised voices.

Mum gasps. 'It's coming from next door,' she whispers. 'The Morrises'.'

I definitely need to convince Jasmine to stay away from Owen. How can I make her see?

There's the sound of breaking crockery. Mum jumps and stifles a shriek. Now there are furious bellows. A man with a boozy slur to his voice. Mum clutches my arm as we remain frozen on the landing, our breaths held.

After several minutes, Mum straightens. 'This is ridiculous. I'm calling the police.'

I grab her sleeve and shake my head. *If they find out it was us . . .*

'Megan, there are kids in there.'

She shakes me off and patters downstairs. Her bare feet make a quiet sucking sound on the floorboards as she walks across the hallway. Mum picks up the phone.

I bang on the wall at the top of the stairs to get her attention. Mum huffs, but looks up. I point in the direction of Owen's house. It's stopped.

Mum hesitates, the phone halfway to her ear. She cocks her

head like a spaniel, then nods once. 'All right then.' Mum wraps her arms round her waist and tries to suppress a shudder. 'I don't like it, living next door to that lot. They're dangerous, Megan. You never know what they're going to do next.'

You think they're dangerous, Mum. If only you knew what I'm capable of.

CHAPTER SEVEN

Dear Hana,

I really need you right now. There's this new girl at Barcham Green: Jasmine. We're getting on so well, but I'm afraid of messing up again.

The thing is, I think Jasmine and I could become really close. Not that she'd ever replace you or anything. You never have to worry about that.

I'm not sure it even matters. She won't want to be my friend if she finds out who I really am.

Part of me wants to push her away, to protect her, but I feel different when I'm with her – so much happier. Is it really selfish of me to want to keep her as a friend, even if I end up hurting her?

I'm going round in circles. I'm sick of being stuck in my own head. I wish you were here to tell me what to do.

I wish for a lot of things. I wish it hadn't ended badly between us.

I miss you. I'm sorry.

Megan xxx

CHAPTER EIGHT

Thirty-three, thirty-four, thirty-five … Where is she? I can't wait much longer. We'll miss the bus. One of my hands taps a nervous rhythm on the back of the door, while the other is poised above the handle, ready to throw it open the second Jasmine rings the bell. The clock continues to tick, counting down every second that makes us more and more late.

Maybe Jasmine's bored of me. Maybe she's not coming at all. I'm surprised by how crushed I feel. Are those tears in my eyes?

'Megan? What are you still doing here?'

I make sure I blink a couple of times before I turn round. Mum's frowning, her fingers rubbing together as if she's making a roll-up. I bet she thinks I'm agoraphobic now. That would be all we need!

'Shall I get the notepad?' she asks, hurrying into the living room to rummage through old TV magazines and Sunday newspapers.

The bell rings. Finally! I wrench the door open and catch a brief glimpse of Jasmine's smile and her flushed cheeks before my eyes lower. She's breathing heavily and blurts something about her hairdryer breaking and having to fight to use Lily's. I don't care. She's here. I want to hug her.

Mum is at the door in a matter of milliseconds. She seems to have forgotten that she's wearing last night's pink eye cream and a dressing gown with a cigarette burn on the sleeve. 'Hello,' she says. 'Who are you?'

'I'm Jasmine. You must be Megan's mum. Great to meet you.'

Jasmine extends a hand for Mum to shake. Mum couldn't look more surprised if Jasmine had a tin opener on the end of her arm. 'Oh ... well ... I didn't know Megan had a new friend.' She shoots me a disgruntled look, then smiles and returns Jasmine's handshake. 'Nice to meet you, too. So your family has just moved into the house on Willingham?'

'Yes, that's right, but how did you—?'

'I work in the café. I hear all the gossip! Where is it you're from? Crete?'

Jasmine needs little prompting to launch into her spiel. 'Cyprus. My mum's Cypriot but my dad's English so I grew up ...' She trails off when she sees me checking my watch. 'Megan's right. We're going to be late. Sorry, Mrs Thomas. Can we chat another time?'

Mum shrieks with laughter. 'Please don't call me Mrs Thomas! You make me sound oooold.' She rolls the 'o' around her tongue like it's a boiled sweet. 'Besides, I'm not married. Call me Angela.'

'Fine. See you soon!' Jasmine heads down the road, waving at my mum. Mum waves back, then shuts the door.

Outside the Morrises', Owen's dad is standing amongst the mess in his front garden: a deckchair with a hole in the bottom, a couple of wheel-less bikes and a bashed-up car bonnet. He looks unshaven and angry. As we walk past, I keep my eyes trained on the pavement.

I hear the door open, then Owen saying something to his dad. Seconds later, he jogs up to us. His hair looks fuzzy without gel in it, and there are dark circles beneath his eyes, but otherwise, he looks OK. Better than OK, if Jasmine's expression is anything to go by. He's wearing a pair of low-slung jeans which hang off his slim hips, and a tight red T-shirt.

'All right?' he says, lighting a cigarette.

'Hi,' Jasmine replies.

Owen walks beside us. Smoke coils through the air, catching in my throat. I swallow a cough. I don't want him to think I'm making a point.

'What you been up to?' he asks.

'Not much. Just school and stuff.'

'You could forget school today. Hang around here?'

Jasmine smiles. 'I can't.'

'Why not?'

'Just can't.'

'All right. Some other time.'

She gives him a coy smile. 'Maybe.'

Jasmine and Owen head down Dog Poo Alley. Owen obviously wants to show off his handiwork. I hesitate, then follow. They turn the corner ahead of me and I hear Owen swear. I catch up just in time to see him punch the fence. Jasmine flinches. I take a step towards her, my muscles tensed.

'Whoever did this is dead!' he bellows, storming past without even looking at me.

Someone has smothered Owen's graffiti in dark red paint. It's been slapped on so thick it's dribbled down the fence. It looks like blood. I try to swallow, but there's a lead weight on my Adam's apple. Who would do this? None of the other graffiti has been touched.

Jasmine raises a shaking hand to her mouth. I grab my notebook and write to her: *Don't worry. This isn't about you. Owen isn't exactly Mr Popular around here.*

Jasmine stares blankly at me. It takes her a while to find the words. 'Thanks, but you're wrong. This *is* about me, Megan.'

I want to ask what she means, but the look on her face tells me to leave it.

I stare at the note I've just written. My handwriting used to be neat, with round, springy lettering. Now I write fast, trying to match the speed of my thoughts. A scrawled scribble. A hopeless alternative for a voice.

I imagine what it would be like to talk to Jasmine. I wonder how my voice would sound. Probably like a gate with rusted hinges – creaky and stiff. Perhaps I've neglected it so long it's rotted away, and I'll never be able to use it again.

We hurry to the war memorial, where the bus is just about to pull away. Jasmine flags it down and the driver stops, fixing us with a dark scowl as we clamber on.

Sadie's out of her seat straight away, blocking the aisle. 'I'm sorry. There's nowhere to sit. You're too late.'

Jasmine grits her teeth. 'Not today.'

Sadie doesn't move.

'You kids need to sit down!' the driver yells.

'Please, just let us past,' Jasmine says firmly. 'I don't want a fight.'

Lindsay seems to come from nowhere, her nose inches from Jasmine's. 'I do,' she whispers menacingly.

Jasmine meets her eyes. There aren't many people who would have the nerve to do that. 'Right, that's it!' Jasmine shouts, trying to push past Lindsay. 'If you don't back off, both of you, I'm going to report you. I said I don't want a fight. I just want to keep my head down and get my exams done, with no hassle.'

'Well, your family should've thought about that before they started stealing other people's jobs,' Lindsay snarls.

The driver's voice booms down the aisle. 'Sit down or I stop the bus!'

'C'mon, Linds,' Sadie says. 'So not worth it.'

But Lindsay doesn't back down.

'Did you hear what I said?' Sadie hisses, pinching her small fingers around Lindsay's arm.

Lindsay wrenches her gaze from Jasmine. When she looks at Sadie, her expression is riddled with ... what? With a jolt, I realise what it is. Fear. Why would Lindsay be afraid of one of her best friends?

They let us pass. Jasmine throws herself into the nearest seat and moves over so I can sit next to her. Lindsay and Sadie deliberately take their time to return to their places.

'I shouldn't have done that, Megan,' Jasmine whispers. 'I shouldn't have lost it with them. I've probably made things worse.'

I scribble *Lindsay?* on an old chewing gum wrapper.

'Apparently the job my mum got had been promised to Lindsay's dad. I get why she's angry, but what am I supposed to do about it?'

I sigh. That is awkward.

Jasmine is quiet for most of the journey. I sit stiffly next to her. I don't really know what to do. I write to her, ask if she's OK, but she just shrugs, so I ask her to tell me about her family in Cyprus. Jasmine grins and starts to talk, bobbing up like a cork in water. I try to concentrate on what she's saying, but I keep noticing a dark, perfectly curved eyelash that's resting on her cheek.

In the end, I look away so I can listen properly. I learn about Aunt Talia, who is fiercely religious and blesses everything, and spoiled cousins Nikos and Theo, who emigrated to London several years ago. Also *Yiayiá* (Grandma), who lives with a parrot in a beautiful mountain village, miles from anywhere, and refuses to move because she wants to walk to her husband's grave every day.

*

Jasmine, Luke and I eat lunch together. Jasmine's picking at a tuna salad that looks like it's seen better days. I offer to share my crisps, but she just shakes her head and says, 'I'm trying to be good.' She gets a wicked glint in her eyes. 'I'll probably ruin it all later by scoffing a massive bar of chocolate! The chocolate here is *so* much better than the stuff in Cyprus. And the choice! I probably inhale about a thousand calories by just standing there and gawping at it!'

I smile. Luke and Jasmine start chatting about sailing. I watch them, wondering if he fancies her. Then I realise Jasmine's talking to me. 'Sorry, Megan. This is really boring. You probably don't have a clue what we're on about! Let's talk about something else.'

She's trying to draw me into the conversation, even though I can't join in. No one else bothers to do that. A trail of goosebumps prickles up my arm.

They start discussing books that have been turned into films, and I lay my jotter on the table so I can jump in from time to time. Luke and I have a fight about *Always Looking North*. I loved the book, hated the film. He's the other way round. Luke ends up stealing my pen and scribbling all over my notepad. I gasp, grab the pen back and draw on his arm. His response is to tear out the sheet and rip it to pieces.

'Stop flirting, you two!' Jasmine laughs.

I blush and look away. We weren't. I don't even know how to flirt. It's the kind of thing Hana was good at, not me. I remember the time she and Luke started a rubber-band fight on the bus. It was a sunny Friday afternoon, the end of term, and they were almost hysterical. I ignored them, staring out of the window as I wondered if they were flirting or just mucking around. When I asked Hana later, she brushed it off, saying they weren't anything more than friends, but I wasn't convinced that was how Luke saw it.

'You OK, Megan?' Jasmine asks, lightly touching my hand. 'I was only teasing.' She catches her lower lip in her teeth. 'You're not offended, are you?'

She looks so worried. I can't believe she cares that much about offending me! How could I have thought I might be able to push her away?

You're no good for her.

But it's too late to back out now.

I spend Saturday on the sofa with Mum, watching a load of rom-coms and stuffing ourselves with sweets. I wish there were other things we could do together, but the choices are kind of limited, thanks to me.

On Sunday morning, the phone rings. Mum natters for a bit, then finds me in my room. 'That was Jasmine.'

Jasmine!

'She says do you want to catch a bus into Bournemouth to do some shopping?'

A smile breaks across my face. Mum grins back. 'I take it that's a yes.'

The last person I went clothes shopping with was Hana,

and she only went to trendy, independent shops, definitely no chains. I never had as much cash as her, so I'd be left sitting outside the changing room while she tried on outfit after outfit.

Shopping with Jasmine is way more fun. We play this game where we pick the most outrageous and hideous things for the other to try on. Jasmine is a bit funny about me knowing her size, but she soon gets over it when she chooses a fluorescent yellow tracksuit for me, complete with leopard-print heels and a bright orange sweatband.

When I make her try an over-the-top silver dress, covered in horrible ruffles, Jasmine shyly lets me into her changing room to see it.

'It's too tight,' she complains, crossing her arms over her stomach.

But I barely notice. I'm fascinated by a little mole on Jasmine's shoulder. It's exactly the same shape as a fir cone.

'Hey, how about this?' Jasmine giggles, pairing the dress with a green rain mac.

I laugh and give her the thumbs up.

At the end of the day, we go for a burger. As we eat, Jasmine checks out the cool new hoodie and purple canvas shoes she's bought.

'Are you sure about the hoodie? It doesn't make me look like a lump?'

I shake my head emphatically.

'Shame you didn't get anything, Megan. You really did look hot in those jeans. You should've got them.'

There's no way I could've afforded the jeans. I felt bad enough asking Mum for a tenner for the bus fare and food.

Jasmine moans about her burger with every mouthful, though it's obvious she's enjoying it.'I really shouldn't be eating this. I'm never going to be an actress if I don't lose weight.'

I frown, grab a napkin and write: *What are you talking about? You don't need to lose weight.*

She reddens.'I just feel massive, you know?'

Well, you're not, I insist, underlining it twice. *You look great.*

Jasmine quickly changes the subject and starts to make up stories about other people in the burger place.'That bloke trims his toenails by biting them ... That couple are on a first date; he likes her, but she keeps checking out the Indian guy behind the till ...'

We're so busy messing about, we almost miss the last bus home, and have to run through the rain to catch it. By the time we board the bus, we're out of breath, soaking wet, and helpless with laughter.

I dream that Jasmine is on the edge of a ridge, looking over her shoulder at me. Her eyes are wide and fearful. Sadie stands behind her, ready to push the small of Jasmine's back and send her plummeting over the edge. Grace is there too, as quiet as ever, but she fixes me with a look that smoulders with anger.

'All you have to do is ask,' Sadie sings.'Just one word to save her life. Why won't you do that for your friend?'

I shake my head. *I can't.*

Grace's eyes narrow: *You can talk,* they say. *I know you can.*

Sadie presses her hand further into Jasmine's back. 'If you don't talk, she'll die. All you have to do is say just ... one ... word.'

Jasmine whimpers, her eyes begging me to help. I start to cry. Great, wracking sobs. *Please don't hurt her. Please!*

'You can save her, Megan. You're just choosing not to,' Sadie says with a smug grin.

Grace takes a step towards me, her jaw clenched. She thinks I'm selfish. Cruel. Cowardly.

No, no, I'm not. I just can't. Please don't take her away from me!

But Sadie is slowly shaking her head, as if she's disappointed. Her elbow juts out as she pulls back her hand and thumps it into Jasmine, who pitches forward in slow motion, arms wheeling, before hurtling out of sight.

I open my eyes. I'm on my bed. Can't breathe. Can't move. I tell myself to turn on the light, but my arm is locked. Why can't I move?

Because you're weak. Pathetic.

A strangled sound escapes from my mouth. I try to stop it, but it scratches across my throat, tears a trail over my tongue.

My fingers twitch. I can move! I swipe a hand through the darkness and it collides with my lamp, which crashes to the floor. I fumble for the switch. Finally, it clicks and light sweeps away the shadows.

Nausea rolls around my stomach. I gulp in more air, trying to slow my thumping heart.

I just about make it to the bathroom before I'm sick. I lean against the toilet bowl, blood roaring in my ears.

A cold hand rests on the back of my neck. 'You OK?' Mum mumbles, her head turned away from the smell.

I don't respond.

You're evil.

'Megan?' Mum asks. 'Are you all right?'

I nod. My brain thuds around like a ping-pong ball.

You deserve to be punished.

'Are you going to be sick again?' Mum asks, taking a step back.

I flush the toilet.

'Do you want some water or mouthwash or something?'

I shake my head.

'How about heartburn tablets? Think I've got some in the cabinet.'

I shake my head again, almost smiling. Mum thinks that any illness can be solved with heartburn tablets.

'All right,' she says softly. 'I'll just go back to bed then.'

I know what she wants. She wants to be a mumsy mum: the type who would tuck me into bed with a kiss and a cup of hot chocolate. But that's not her. I'm OK with that. I just wish she was.

Mum pats the top of my head and returns to her bedroom,

but doesn't quite pull the door shut. I hear her open the window, then there's the flick of a lighter. She'll spray deodorant afterwards, thinking it will mask the smell.

I stumble back to my room and into bed. Remnants of the dream buzz around me like wasps. Every time I close my eyes, I see the look on Jasmine's face, just before she fell. I know what she was thinking: *You betrayed me.*

CHAPTER NINE

When my alarm goes off the next morning, my eyelids are leaden and there's a slow beat drumming on my temples. I wrench my eyes open but everything is unfocused. I can't have had more than a couple of hours' sleep. I wait for my vision to clear before shuffling into the corridor.

The bathroom door is open and a cloud of lemon-scented steam is curling out. Mum's standing in front of the mirror with a towel wrapped around her, pulling odd faces as she puts mascara on.

When Mum sees me watching, she starts to talk, but her voice hasn't quite woken up yet. She clears her throat and tries again. 'Are you still ill? Do you want me to call school?' She looks at me properly and actually gasps. 'Look at the state of you! You can't go out like that!' She reaches out to try to flatten my hair.

I jerk away from her.

'Oh, come on, I'm only joking!' And she laughs, just to prove it.

Ha bloody ha.

Mum stops laughing and her eyes harden so fast they almost crack. 'Fine,' she snaps. 'Are you staying or going, because I've got to leave for work. Make your mind up quickly.'

I'm so tired. I just can't face it today. I point to my bed.

Mum nods once, then heads downstairs.

'I'll ring Jasmine's mum too,' she says. 'Tell her not to call for you today.'

I wake mid-morning. My room feels stuffy so I push the window open, taking deep breaths of the air that wafts inside, bringing the scent of rain with it.

I spend the day flicking through rubbish on TV. I'm on my fifth episode of some dining/dating show when Mum comes through the door. She calls out, 'Hiya. I was let off a bit early because we were quiet. Have you been sick again?'

I reach for the remote, my arm heavy and languid. I mute the TV, lift my head and shake it at her.

Mum looks mischievous. 'You've got a visitor!' she announces.

What? Please don't tell me you mean Jasmine!

I've been in these pyjamas all day. I didn't even bother to have a shower this morning. My skin feels greasy, my hair lank. I *so* don't want her seeing me like this!

Jasmine's earrings tinkle as she pokes her head round the door. 'Hi! How are you feeling? What is it? Stomach bug? Or did you eat something bad? We went to this Chinese buffet in

Cyprus. Oh my God, Megan, I was so ill. I can't even touch prawns now. Just the thought of them makes me queasy. At least, I think it was the prawns. There was this beef dish as well . . . I'm not sure.'

'I think she'll be OK to go back tomorrow,' Mum says. 'I don't think I can keep her in another day. She's like a wild animal – always wants to be outside!'

Great. Thanks for that, Mum.

Jasmine grins. I manage a flicker of a smile in return, then retreat behind my hair.

Mum ushers Jasmine into the living room, then hovers just outside the door as she takes off her coat and shoes.

Jasmine sinks into the sofa next to me. I breathe in her lovely, incensey smell. She taps her lap. 'Do you want to put your feet up?'

A blush devours my face and I shake my head.

'Come on, silly.' Jasmine laughs, pulls my legs up and rests them across her thighs. I stare in horror at the pink bunny rabbits dancing across my pyjamas, but Jasmine doesn't seem to notice.

'I sat with Luke on the bus today. He was telling me what you were like, you know, before . . . ' Her words trail off, then she says, 'I wish I'd known you then.'

I look away.

'Fancy a cuppa, Jasmine?' Mum asks.

Jasmine nods. The moment Mum leaves, she leans forward eagerly. 'Someone was waiting for me at the bus stop tonight.' She lets a pause hang for a few dramatic seconds, before gushing, 'It was Owen!'

I stiffen.

'I mean, I'm quite flattered that he likes me, but I'm not sure how I feel about him. I don't know if the whole rebel thing is sexy or scary.'

Scary. Definitely scary. And he's blatantly just interested in one thing.

As soon as I think it, I feel bad. There are loads of reasons why boys would be interested in Jasmine. I'm just bitter.

You're a cow.

I jump. Breathe. Tell myself to act normal.

Jasmine misreads my expression. 'Don't you think he's good-looking?'

I snort.

'Does that mean you don't?'

I shrug. I'm no good at this type of thing.

Mum rushes in. I wonder how long she's been eavesdropping. 'Oh, that whole family's a bad lot. Dad went to prison, you know,' she utters in a scandalised whisper. 'I'm telling you, Jasmine, some of the things we've heard through the walls … Well, just steer clear of him if you want my advice. He's trouble.'

For once I'm grateful for Mum's loose tongue.

Jasmine doesn't know what to say. She pauses, then offers Mum a vague smile. 'Thanks for the warning. I'll think about it.'

'Do you want to stay for dinner?' Mum asks. 'Don't worry, I'll make Megan have a shower first.'

For God's sake! I'm not five!

Jasmine smiles. 'That would be great, thanks. I'll just text my parents.'

Mum leaves and the microwave starts to hum in the kitchen.

Jasmine whips round, her eyes shining. 'Guess what?' she whispers, casting a quick glance behind to make sure Mum's not there. 'Owen asked if we want to meet them in Lyndhurst on Friday night.'

I'm already shaking my head.

'Oh come on, Megan. Please. It'll be fun! He's going to get us some booze and we'll just hang out in the park.'

Brilliant. So he wants to get you drunk. This is a bad, bad idea. We can't go. No way.

'There'll be boys there. Owen's mates.'

As if that will convince me!

'Or bring Luke if you like.'

I don't think so.

'Don't make me go alone, Megan.'

Alone? You can't go alone.

Jasmine pouts. How can I be angry with her when she looks like that?

You're not leaving me much of a choice.

She sees me wavering and makes one last effort. 'Pleeeeaaaase!'

OK. But I'm not drinking. And I'm not going any further than Lyndhurst. Even for you.

I nod, feeling slightly sick. Jasmine stifles a squeal as she claps her hands together. 'It's going to be great, I promise! You tell your mum you're at mine, and I'll tell my parents I'm at yours! We'll get the last bus back to Brookby at half eleven.'

She's already planned it out. Despite myself, I smile.

On Friday, Jasmine and I huddle together on a dark street. It's a cold, damp night and the bus is late. Lindsay and Josh are a few feet away. They're so engrossed in each other, they don't even realise we're here.

I don't know Lindsay that well. In primary school, our little gang consisted of me, Hana, Sadie and Grace. But it all changed when we started secondary school. It was just Sadie and Grace for a year or so, until Lindsay showed up. Then the three of them were inseparable. I can see why Sadie wanted Jasmine to join the group – four was always a good number.

It's strange to see Lindsay without Sadie. I wonder if they're all meeting somewhere. God, I hope they're not coming to the park with us. No, that wouldn't happen. Everyone knows that Sadie and Owen haven't spoken since their break-up in the summer.

I try not to stare at them. It's really hard! Jasmine sniggers and tries to disguise it as a cough.

Lindsay disentangles herself. 'What you staring at?'

'Nothing,' Jasmine says coolly, moving a little further down the road.

'Yeah. You'd better not be. Don't think you can steal my man, like your mum stole my dad's job. I'm watching you, new girl.'

'Welcome to Brookby,' Jasmine mutters, 'where everyone's so friendly.'

I rub her shoulder and she manages a quick smile. Jasmine's

wearing a short denim skirt and leather boots. Her large earrings tumble through her hair: two tear-shaped amber stones hanging above several silver twists. Every few minutes, she tugs at her skirt self-consciously. I wish I could tell her how nice she looks.

I find my phone and hold it up to take a selfie. We put our heads together, grinning like idiots, then blink away the dots of light after the flash. I study the photo. I look so pasty next to Jasmine. My hair falls in unruly waves, in contrast to her tight curls. My eyes just seem dull next to the rich brown of hers.

Jasmine points at the bus trundling towards us. 'Finally. About bloody time.'

Inside, the heating's on, but we're both frozen, so we shuffle close together. I shut my eyes, enjoying the feeling of her warm body against mine, trying to forget where we're going and who we're meeting.

Jasmine nudges me and I open my eyes.'Look what I've got,' she says with an impish grin, holding up a bottle of water.

I frown. What's so special about water?

'It's Archers and lemonade, Megan.'

I blush. I'm such an idiot!

'Want some?'

I shake my head, my stomach lurching.

'Go on!'

Jasmine takes a swig, then waves it under my nose. I get a sickly-sweet whiff of peaches and lemon. I wonder how much is Archers and how much is lemonade. It smells pretty strong.

You don't know what I'm like when I'm drunk.

I pull my notepad out and scribble: *I don't drink.*

'But you have drunk before, right?'

I nod, wincing slightly. *Please don't drag that up. Just don't.*

'Then you know it'll make you feel good. Help you relax.'

I said no! I think, turning away. *I can't, OK? I can't lose control. Stop pushing.*

'All right,' she says quickly. 'Sorry. It's up to you. Guess I'll have to drink both of these myself.' Jasmine pulls another bottle from her bag, her eyes glinting.

There's a flutter of panic in my chest. I can't let her drink both! She'll be wasted. I bet Owen would love that. I grab the unopened bottle.

'Yes! Good girl!'

But I shove it straight in my bag.

Jasmine sighs. Great. She thinks I'm boring now. I'm completely spoiling her night.

Why does she bother with you?

'If you're not going to drink it, can I have it back, please?' Jasmine asks, her voice flat. She's going to ditch me as soon as we get there. I'll be left behind, just like before. All because I can't let go.

'Megan?' Jasmine asks, a trace of irritation in her voice.

No. I won't let you drink all that on your own.

I yank the bottle out of my bag, unscrew the lid in a few rapid, jerky movements, and take a massive gulp before I can change my mind. The Archers stings my throat. It almost comes back up again, but I make myself swallow. Jasmine grins, then drinks some more.

Half an hour later, when we reach Lyndhurst, my bottle is empty and my head feels fuzzy. Jasmine's got this happy, dazed expression on her face and I'm pretty sure I look the same. We get up just before the bus stops, swaying and giggling down the aisle, arms linked to stop each other from toppling over.

Outside, it doesn't seem as cold any more. I keep my arm hooked through Jasmine's. Not just to steady myself. I like it. I'm having fun now. I wonder what the hell I was worrying about. I wonder why Mr Harwell doesn't prescribe alcohol to help me relax, instead of stupid breathing exercises.

We stagger up the High Street, towards the park where we're meeting Owen. Dunno where Lindsay and Josh went – must've gone the other way. Unless they were too busy snogging on the back seat and missed the stop!

We take a load of comedy pictures on my phone. One with Jasmine flaring her nostrils, one of me crossing my eyes. One of the ladder in Jasmine's tights, which is so, so funny, even though we don't know why.

Can't believe how dizzy I am! Mustn't drink any more. But Jasmine's right. I'm so chilled out now. I'm never chilled out. It feels good.

We reach the park gates and Jasmine drops my arm to wave at someone. I hold back, my nerves sobering me, as she weaves across the path. There are several lads and a couple of girls standing beneath a lamp, their cigarette smoke wafting up into the orange light.

'All right?' Owen peels off from the group and saunters towards Jasmine. Cocky bastard! 'Want a drink?'

'Yeah, what have you got?'

'Vodka.'

'Fine. Great.'

I wonder if Jasmine's ever had vodka before. I haven't.

'OK with you, Megan?' Jasmine asks, looking back at me. She gives me a reassuring smile and holds out her hand. Without hesitation, I step forward and take it.

Owen introduces us to the others, though Jasmine has to remind him what my name is. 'Megan's your next-door neighbour and you don't even know her name!' She giggles.

I blush. I feel like she's laughing at me.

Owen stands really close to Jasmine, making sure everyone knows he's interested. One of his mates winks and throws him a leery look. I loop my arm through Jasmine's again, pretending I'm cold.

Jasmine asks, 'Where's this vodka, then?'

Someone hands her a bottle with a cheap-looking label. She takes a tentative sip, then her face screws up. Jasmine hands me the bottle. There's a lipstick smudge around the rim that's not hers. It makes me feel sick, but I resist the urge to wipe it off. What am I doing? I promised I'd never drink again. I swore.

The others are looking at me. 'Go on,' Jasmine whispers. I don't want to embarrass her, so I drink.

It's foul! Don't spit it out, Megan. Keep it down. Swallow. That's right. Just swallow.

I force it down. It blazes a hot trail through my windpipe

before settling in my stomach. Actually, now it's there, it doesn't feel so bad. Warm. Comforting. Maybe, in a bit, I'll have some more.

I can't stop laughing. I dunno why I'm laughing. Can't remember. The ground is moving, but I don't care. I don't care about anything. I just feel so good. So happy. And everything's hilarious.

Are there trees in the park? I don't remember. Doesn't matter. I like trees. Trees are my friends. I'm going to hug one.

'Megan!' Jasmine shrieks from somewhere in the darkness. 'What you doing? Tree-hugger! Hippy!' She grabs my hand. 'C'mon.'

Jasmine's hand is nice. I want to hold it all the time.

'Owen wants to show us this really cool place.'

Owen. Oh yeah. I remember. Sort of. He drove us here. His driving's crazy. I was almost sick.

'C'mon! He wants to show us.'

Show us what? I can't see anything! It's too bloody dark!

Just trees. Loadsa loadsa trees. Where are we? Whatever. I don't care. I like being with the trees.

'This way, hurry up.'

What? You want me to climb a hill? I'll fall over!

Shadowy figures in front. Follow the torch.

Slow down, Jasmine. My legs aren't working!

We stop at the top. Ha! That rhymes. Stop at the top.

The moon pokes over the trees. I see now. See Jasmine. I

want to kiss her. Weird. Where did that come from? Kiss her? What you on about? You're drunk.

'Look,' Jasmine says, pointing.

I look.

Every scrap of air leaves my lungs.

No. We can't be. Not here. I . . . I can't be here.

My head clears a little. I stumble.

I can't. I can't. I can't.

A faint voice. 'Megan? What is it? What's wrong?'

We're on the wrong side of Lyndhurst.

We're at the ridge.

The place I've avoided for the last seven months.

Because it's where Hana died.

CHAPTER TEN

What the . . . ? Where am I? God, my head. I feel so rough.

I can tell by the way I'm being jolted around that I'm in the back of a car. My shoulder aches, my hand is grazed and grubby, my head's spinning. Whose car am I in? Where am I? Why am I so confused?

Then I hear Jasmine's voice. And it all comes back. Owen. Vodka. The ridge. I hear some sort of groan, but the sound doesn't belong to me. It's like a wounded dog.

Jasmine whips round from the front seat. 'Megan? God, Megan, are you OK? You fainted. Scared the crap out of me! Don't worry, Owen carried you to his car. He's taking us home.'

I sit up. Darkness creeps into the corner of my eyes, like I might pass out again.

'S'OK. Just relax. You're going to be fine.' Jasmine's words slur into a stream of noise.

Wait a minute. Home? I can't go home! Mum can't see me like this!

I peer at the numbers on the car's clock. They swim around. I blink. Refocus. 00:05.

All right. That's all right. Mum will be in bed.

Jasmine's eyes are wide, anxious. 'I'm sorry. I'm really sorry. I shouldn't have dragged you out. This is all my fault.'

Sorry? You're sorry? I've spent months trying to forget, to scrub the memory away, but you took me there, of all places! How could you?

'Please don't be cross with me.' Jasmine's voice breaks. I block it out, ignore her hurt. *You have no right to be upset when you've put me through this!*

I roll over so I don't have to look at her. I feel like my body keeps rolling, over and over again. I close my eyes.

Twenty nauseating minutes later, the car stops. An icy gust of wind hits my legs when Owen opens the door. He leans over me, his face grim. What's that on his nose? Looks like scratches. Recent. Dotted with drops of blood.

'Yeah, that's right. You did that!' he shouts. 'Should've left you there, you little—'

'Hey, that's enough!' Jasmine says, stepping between us.

I did that to his face? No. I can't have done.

Vicious bitch!

'It's OK, Megan,' Jasmine says, reaching for me. 'You just freaked out a bit when he tried to pick you up.'

I snatch my hand away. That's not OK! Why don't I remember it? Why did he take us there in the first place? He knows that's where Hana . . . Was he trying to mess with me? Does he know the truth? Was he trying to get me to talk?

I lean over, retching.

'Don't get any puke in my car!' Owen yells.

Jasmine quickly sweeps my hair out of my face. Nothing comes up, though.

Gripping the handle, I hoist myself out of the car. My legs can barely hold my weight. Owen slams the door, jumps in the front, then revs the engine, flying off with a screeching wheel spin. I *really* hope that hasn't woken Mum up.

Jasmine sighs. 'I guess he's going back out again. I think we might have blown it. I'll text him tomorrow, smooth things over.'

What's this 'we'? I never wanted anything to do with him in the first place! Hang on – you have his phone number?

'Megan?' Jasmine says in a small voice. 'Can I stay? I'm worried about you. I know it wasn't just the drink that made you faint. I saw your face when you realised where we were. I know Owen knows something, but I want to hear it from you. Please, will you try to explain?'

I shake my head and dig around my pocket for my keys.

'Fine. Let's not talk about it tonight. But can I at least stay?'

Another head shake. Jasmine's eyes well with tears. I look away.

'If that's what you want, I'll go. But I'm coming back tomorrow.'

Deep beneath the anger, something stirs within me. But I'm too tired and weak to identify it.

I listen as Jasmine walks away, then draw a deep breath, focus on the key and try to steady my hand. I just have to make it to bed without waking Mum. The latch clicks. I push the door open and a creak cuts through the sleepy stillness inside. At least everything's dark. I peer into the living room. Mum's not asleep on the sofa, which is good.

I turn on the hallway light. Next to the coat hook is this cheap print of a sunset over a beach. Mum got a discount because there's an imperfection: a splotch of black in the upper right corner. She joked at the time – said it could be a bird or something. But it isn't a bird. It clearly isn't a bird! I want to tear the picture down, smash it to pieces. I wrench it off the hook and raise it above my head, my teeth locked, arms shaking. Then this noise sort of drops out of my mouth: a sob. I slide down the wall, put the picture facedown next to me, lean my head against my knees, and cry.

When I manage to get myself together, I look around as if I don't know where I am. The last couple of hours seem unreal. But my thudding head and bruised skin say otherwise. My tongue is furry, mouth thick with the taste of something I don't recognise.

I head for the kitchen, fingers trailing along the walls to support me. Tea. I need tea. I fumble with the mug and teabag. My fingers are fat and clumsy.

I sit at the table and take a sip. Searing heat almost blisters my lip. It's still boiling hot! I haven't added any milk.

What's wrong with me?

I'm still a bit drunk. That's what it is. I just need to go to bed. Pretend this whole night never happened.

I drag myself up the stairs – on all fours at one point – and flop into bed, fully clothed.

I'm woken in the morning by Mum opening my door. 'Megan? What are you doing here? Didn't you stay at Jasmine's? What time did you get in? Why are you still dressed? Why has my picture been taken off the wall?'

I roll over and ignore her. Too many questions. Too early to answer.

But she perches on the edge of my bed. 'Hey, I'm talking to you.'

I groan. My brain seems to be stuffed with marshmallow. I feel sick, too. Without turning to look at her, I hold out my hand.

Mum understands, finds the notepad I always keep on my bedside table, and gives it to me.

I write: *We had a fight.*

'What about?'

I shake my head.

She huffs and stomps out, muttering something about 'stroppy teenagers'.

The next time I wake, I catch the sound of voices downstairs. I creep on to the landing and peek around the banister. Mum and Jasmine are talking near the front door. I guess that means Jasmine's parents didn't find out we were drinking, or she'd definitely be grounded.

I'm not ready to face Jasmine yet. I sit on the top step. They're the other side of the stairs so they won't see me, but I can hear them clearly.

'She's still sleeping, Jasmine.' Mum's voice is clipped. 'What happened last night? Megan got in really late.'

'We had a fight,' Jasmine says carefully. 'I'm not really sure why. We went up to the ridge and she just . . .'

'What?' Mum snaps. 'Where did you go?'

'T-to the ridge. The other side of Lyndhurst.'

'Oh, God,' Mum groans. 'You don't know what happened, do you? Who were you with? Bloody kids. They should've known better.'

'What? What happened there?'

Mum pauses, then asks, 'Has Megan even mentioned Hana?'

Don't say her name! Please . . . just . . . don't.

I squeeze my eyes shut. Too late. A couple of tears sneak out, like the first scattered raindrops before a storm. There's a couple more. Then they become a downpour. I clamp my hand over my mouth to muffle my cries. I wrap the other hand around the banister and clutch it until my knuckles go white.

'I heard rumours that a girl from Brookby died last summer,' Jasmine explains. 'Then Luke told me she was Megan's best friend, and that Megan hasn't spoken since she died.'

Mum sighs. 'It sounds like you already know most of it.'

'I don't really know how she died. The details. Luke just said there was an accident.'

'Well . . .' Mum draws out the word as if she can postpone her answer. 'Megan, Hana and some other kids were at the ridge. I don't know what they were doing, mucking around on a rope swing or something, but there was an accident and Hana fell.'

Hana fell. She fell. She died.

I can't ... There's too much. Agony, horror, rage, guilt. My brain roars with it all.

Jasmine starts to cry too.

What right do you *have to cry? Was she* your *best friend?*

'Why don't you come in?' Mum says. 'I'll see if I can raise Megan, then you can patch things up.'

There's a tiny island of reason in my mind, where I know it's not Jasmine's fault, but the pain is like a tidal wave, flooding and consuming everything.

'No,' Jasmine blurts. 'Thank you. I – I don't think I should. I feel a bit, you know ...'

I hear her backing away, towards the door, then it opens and Jasmine leaves without saying goodbye.

I stand, step forward, and reach out my hand as if I can stop her leaving, without really knowing whether I want her to stay or go.

I mooch around the house for the rest of the day, trying to avoid Mum, who inconveniently has the day off. She corners me at dinner, when I'm forcing down some beans on toast.

'Jasmine came round earlier. She wants to sort things out.'

I don't respond, neatly slicing a corner from my triangle of toast.

'I told her about Hana.'

I pause with the fork halfway to my mouth. I watch it,

unable to meet Mum's eyes. The beans look like maggots swimming in blood. Some of the sauce drips away and one of the beans slides off and drops to the table. I throw the fork down.

'I know it's hard for you, Megan. But she's heard stuff at school, so I thought she should know the truth.'

My breath shakes and judders. *I know, Mum. I should've told her myself.*

Mum frowns.'I'm sorry if I've done the wrong thing. I always put my foot in it.'

No. You did the right thing. I'd rather Jasmine heard it from you than some stupid lies from Sadie.

I reach for the empty can of beans and peel a strip off the label. I write *Thank you* on the back.

Mum smiles and squeezes my hand.'Do my roots for me later? I look like a scarecrow!'

I nod.

Mum gets this sly look on her face.'Maybe we could—'

I shake my head before she's even finished speaking. There's no way I'm letting her loose on my hair.

I don't sleep that night. I alternate between crying into my pillow and drifting through nightmares. I wake late on Sunday morning. My skin feels taut, like I've cried out every last drop of water, wrung myself dry like a dishcloth. I'm too tired to be cross with Jasmine any more. I send her a text:

Will you come over?

When she arrives, just half an hour later, Jasmine's face is pallid, her curls hang limply, and her clothes are creased. We look at each other for a moment, tears welling in both our eyes, then she wraps her arms around me and starts to sob. 'Are you OK? I'm so sorry. I honestly had no idea.'

I glance around for something to write on, but we're standing in the doorway. I don't know how else to reassure her, so I reach out, cup Jasmine's chin in my palm, and give her a weak smile. Something flickers through me. A hazy, drunken memory. A feeling. I try to grab hold of it, but it's like trying to catch a cloud.

'I guess that means I'm forgiven?'

I nod.

Mum totters out of the kitchen. 'Just popping to the shop. I fancy something naughty. You want anything? Chocolate?'

I fix her with a look. I assume 'something naughty' means fags.

'What?' she says, with a wicked grin. 'God, Megan. Sometimes I think you're the mum and I'm the kid!'

I try to smile back, but it falters. Mum lost her own parents in a car accident a couple of years before I was born. She must miss them so much, especially now Gran and Grandpa are gone.

We wave her off, then I lead Jasmine up to my room, tapping the banister in a nervous, staccato rhythm as we mount the stairs.

I stop in the doorway of my bedroom, seeing it through Jasmine's eyes. It's immaculate. All the surfaces are clean and clutter-free, my books are alphabetised, my CDs grouped by genre. I almost want to chuck an old plate on the floor, or leave some dirty socks lying around, to make it seem normal. Jasmine is looking at the walls, though, which are decorated with prints from the Wildlife Photographer of the Year Award.

Early afternoon light slants through my window and highlights drifting dust motes. I watch them for a moment, transfixed, then wrench my eyes away, looking for something else to distract me.

Jasmine's waiting. I have to do this. I almost can't bear to let Hana go again, but she's not here any more, and Jasmine is. Hands shaking, I reach beneath my pillow and pull out a stack ßof letters, all addressed to Hana. All unanswered. I pass them to Jasmine.

I watch while she scans the pages. Her eyes are red, her skin blotchy. I hate seeing her like this.

When Jasmine finishes, she tucks the pile of letters beneath my pillow again. Then she stares at the floor, trying to gather the right words. After a few moments, she seems to give up, and just lunges forward to grab my arms. 'Oh, Megan,' she gushes, 'I'm so sorry. Sorry you lost your best friend. Sorry you had to see it. I wish I could make it all go away. I can't imagine what you've been through.'

Jasmine draws me into a fierce hug, her fingernails digging into my back. I focus on the feel of her chest against mine, the sound of her breath in my ear, the brush of her hair against my neck. A knot of tension in my shoulder blades loosens.

'Do you have any pictures? I'd like to see, if … if that's OK.'

My heart quickens, but I drop to the floor and scrabble around the bottom of my wardrobe for the right photo album. I find it and quickly flick through.

There it is. Hana and I standing in Grandpa's garden, arms wrapped around each other, cheeks pressed together, her grin matching mine. Hana's wearing a black top with glittery stars, paired with some combat shorts that end just above her knees. Everything looked great on her. Even the scruffy Dr Martens were kooky and cute. I bet she was wearing odd socks beneath them. She was the kind of person who'd wear Christmas socks in August.

Jasmine studies the picture. 'You look so happy and comfortable with each other,' she murmurs.

I wish Hana were here. Wish you could meet her.

Tears glisten in Jasmine's eyes. She tries to hold them back, but they overflow and roll down her face. Seconds later, we're both clutching each other again and crying.

'You know it wasn't your fault, right?' Jasmine says, her voice thick with tears. 'You keep saying sorry in your letters, but your mum said it was an accident.'

I pull away from her sharply and stand to look out of the window. *I've told you as much as I can. Don't ask for any more.*

Jasmine starts to say something else, but Mum calls up the stairs. 'Are you two hungry? I'm starving! I could make lunch if you like?'

'Are you hungry?' Jasmine whispers.

I shrug.

'Be right down!' Jasmine calls.

I turn to leave, but Jasmine grabs my hand to stop me. 'Wait. Just a minute. There's something I want to tell you, too. I want to explain why we moved. I know it seems strange. I know people are talking about me, wondering why I came here just before exams.'

I grab my notepad. *You don't have to,* I write.

'But I want you to know.' Jasmine draws in a big breath. 'Some girls at my old school were giving me a really hard time. It was affecting my schoolwork, so Mum and Dad thought I should sit my exams in a new school.'

That's awful, I write. *Who could not like you?*

She gives me a tearful smile.

I'm glad you told me, I add. *I'm glad you moved, even if it was for a horrible reason.*

'Me too.' Jasmine swipes tears from her face and says, 'Right, let's get something to eat!'

The kitchen is thick with the scent of tomato soup. It bubbles away in a pan on the hob, spitting out drops like lava from a volcano.

Mum laughs when she sees me inspecting the can. 'So I didn't technically "make" it. But it'll do, won't it?'

'It's fine,' Jasmine assures her. 'Smells great!'

Jasmine starts chatting about a TV programme where a woman adopts a child who turns out to be her younger sister. Mum asks if she'd like to act in a soap, and Jasmine laughs and says she'd rather be on stage. Then she notices some gossip magazine lying on the table and they start to coo over the male torsos in the centrefold.

I tune out, concentrate on blowing steam off my soup. I'm glad Jasmine knows now. Well, she knows as much as Mum. Neither of them knows the whole truth. What I did to Hana.

The voice screams through my head, splitting it in two.

Murderer.

CHAPTER ELEVEN

Dear Jasmine,

I've taken your advice. I'm not going to write to Hana any more. I like your idea of writing her a goodbye letter, and I will do some day, I promise.

Anyway, I thought, seeing as I won't be writing to her, that maybe I could write to you instead? You were asking about Hana, what she was like. I wanted to think about it, so I could get her just right.

Hana was sarcastic, funny, dry; beautiful, quirky and cool. She was a geek. Massively into *Star Trek*, *Star Wars*, *Stargate*. God, it made her mad when I mixed them up! She hated ferrets, loved gherkins, and once downed a whole bottle of banana FRijj in one go. She was super-smart, and could recite the whole periodic table off the top of her head.

On my sixth birthday, Mum bought me this doll. It was a cheap, knock-off Barbie and its leg kept falling off. I was gutted. I really wanted a Disney Sleeping Beauty Barbie, just like Hana's. So she used all her birthday money, and the pocket money she'd been saving for a new bike basket, to buy me one. She'd do anything to make someone else happy.

I knew her inside out. Better than I knew anyone. I miss her. It still hurts so much.

I wish you could've met her – you would have absolutely loved her.

Megan xxx

CHAPTER TWELVE

Jasmine and I are walking to the bus after school. She's all caught up in this Drama project she's working on, and has barely taken a breath in the last three minutes, until we see Luke ahead. 'What's that on Luke's back?' she asks.

We get a little closer. It's a Post-it note. I sigh when I read the single word on it.

Jasmine gasps. 'Luke!' she shouts. Several people turn round, including Luke. Jasmine starts towards him, but I grab her arm, rummage for my notebook and scribble a message: *Don't tell him. I'll take it off on the bus without him noticing.*

Jasmine nods and we catch up with Luke. 'Er – hi!' Jasmine says with an exaggerated smile. 'Mind if we sit with you on the bus?'

'Nope. Was that … what you wanted?'

'Yeah! Just wanted to make sure we could all sit together.'

We board the bus and find some seats. Luke shoots us an odd look when we sit behind him, instead of across the aisle. He twists round, his back to me, so he can moan to Jasmine about his football coach.

I gently peel the Post-it from Luke's back. I thought I was being subtle, but he whips round and asks what I'm doing. I squeeze the note into a ball. I hope it hasn't been there all day.

'Nothing,' Jasmine says quickly. 'Just some grass on your back.'

Luke glares at my fist. 'Let me see it. I knew something was up today. Those bastards!'

I shake my head.

'Give it to me, Megan,' he demands.

I shake my head again.

Luke grabs my hand and roughly prises it open. He turns away from us to read it, then lets out a growl of frustration and thumps the seat in front.

Jasmine bites her lip.

Luke takes some deep breaths, like he's trying not to lose it.

I wait a few minutes, then give his shoulder a squeeze. He flinches away. I clamber over Jasmine and sit next to him.

They're not worth it, I write.

Luke gives me a half-smile. 'Thanks for trying to get it off. You're not very stealthy though!'

I gasp. *I'm a champion of stealth!* I write. *You must have Spider-Man senses!*

I get a proper smile this time. 'Yeah, that's me. Spider-Man!'

I have an idea. It's impulsive, spur-of-the-moment. So not a Megan idea – which makes me like it even more. *Do you fancy going out for food tonight?* I scribble. *We could try that new place in Lyndhurst, Carino's.*

Luke turns an alarming shade of crimson. 'Yeah, I'd love to!'

I stand up and wave my notepad at Jasmine, pointing to what I've just written. 'That's a genius idea!' she says.

When I turn back to Luke, he's gone all quiet again, and won't look at me. And Mum thinks *my* mood swings are bad! There are a couple of minutes of silence, then Jasmine has us both laughing at a pretty good impression of Mrs Austin, complete with the long, wobbly neck.

After the bus has dropped us off, I make a detour to the café to beg some money from Mum. Her lips tighten, but she says, 'Go on, then. I'll only spend it on fags. Twenty quid do?'

I shake my head and take ten. I'll make it last.

Luke's in Brookby tonight. His parents are separated. Some nights he stays with his dad in the next village, Ashworth, and others he's with his mum, Sandra. He doesn't talk about his dad much, but I get the impression he doesn't like going over there. I think he only does because his dad has shared custody of Simon, and Luke's fairly protective of his little brother.

Luke texts to let us know his mum can bring us home afterwards, and we arrange to meet at the war memorial to catch the bus into town.

Carino's is a really cool place with a chilled-out atmosphere and great music. Our gangly waiter seems quite taken with Jasmine, and we get free garlic bread to share. When he brings it, the waiter makes some rubbish joke about Luke getting all the girls. I think he's fishing to find out if Jasmine is available.

'We're all just friends,' Jasmine says sweetly. When Luke looks down at the menu, she arches an eyebrow at me, but I pretend not to notice.

Luke tries to prove his manliness by scoffing an 'inferno' pizza, but he ends up sweating and having to order a not-so-manly milkshake to soothe his mouth.

'I don't know what you're talking about. It's fine,' Jasmine says, taking a massive bite of Luke's abandoned meal. Luke gives her a really cold look for stealing from his plate, but seconds later, when she's coughing and spitting into a napkin, he and I are both cracking up.

Jasmine declares that she wants to practise some accents for her Drama project. They range from an appalling Scouse, which sounds more like Scottish, to a passable American. She plays games with the besotted waiter, who has absolutely no idea that, every time she speaks to him, she's trying out a different one. I can't look at her, or I'll just collapse into laughter.

As we're leaving, the waiter tells Jasmine she has a lovely voice and asks where she's from. We have to rush outside, where we explode with hysterics.

By the time Sandra arrives, we're all very giddy.

Sandra is a sweet, timid woman. I've known her for years, without really knowing her at all – she's just so shy. Several inches shorter than Luke, she flits around like a nervous little chaffinch.

'You haven't been drinking, have you?' Sandra leans in to sniff Luke's breath, much to his embarrassment. His mood seems to have shifted again and he rounds on his mum when she tries to ask how I am. 'What are you asking her that for? You know Megan can't answer. I told you. Jesus!'

Sandra blushes. Luke storms ahead on the short walk back to the car, and she quietly apologises, saying something about him 'growing more like his father every day'.

At the car, Jasmine not-so-subtly offers to go in the front, so Luke and I can sit in the back. Luke hesitates for a moment, but I think he feels bad for the way he spoke to his mum, so he slips into the passenger seat. He doesn't seem to be very comfortable, and keeps shooting little glances at me and Jasmine.

On the way home, Sandra asks Jasmine a couple of questions about Cyprus. I wonder if she's sizing her up as a potential girlfriend for Luke. I don't know why, but the thought makes me squirm.

Sandra suggests that we take the scenic route back, so Jasmine can see a different part of the forest. Luke grumbles that we won't be able to see anything in the dark, but Jasmine thinks it's a great idea.

We're driving down a narrow, winding country lane when Sandra brakes suddenly. 'Oh, look!' she says, pointing towards a small village green where her headlights are illuminating a herd of deer. The stag stands in the centre, his antlers rising majestically into the night. His breath steams out of his nostrils, forming little clouds of moisture in the air.

I've seen deer at night before, silhouetted against the moonlight, but never so many, and it's never felt so magical. Perhaps it's the expression on Jasmine's face as we watch in rapt silence. Or maybe it's because she grabs my hand and clutches it tightly, as if she wants to check that this is real, that it's actually happening.

After a few minutes, the herd moves on. Jasmine doesn't let go of my hand, and I have a huge grin on my face all the way back to Brookby.

Sandra stops in the High Street to pick up some milk.

'Why don't I walk Megan home?' Luke offers. 'It's not far.'

Sandra looks surprised. 'I can drive you, it's no problem.'

'Er – well, I need a few things in the shop, too,' Jasmine says. 'Don't know how long I'll be. These two might as well get off.'

Get off. My face reddens – I'm glad of the dark.

Luke clears his throat and pretends to study the window controls.

'Head off!' Jasmine says quickly. 'I mean head off!'

As we leave, Jasmine winks at me. I don't know why she keeps going on about the two of us. Luke always liked Hana, not me. Besides, he knows enough about me to understand he's better off not going there.

I've often wondered why we stayed friends, after what happened. I thought it would be too painful, but it's actually kind of comforting to have someone who knows everything. Someone I can trust.

Just imagining for a second that Jasmine's right, I wonder

how I'd feel if he made a move tonight. Weird, probably. God, I hope he doesn't.

Luke starts to tell me about his nephews and how they terrorised the poor babysitter the last time his aunt and uncle went out. The youngest, James, is three. 'He peed all over the bathroom floor. When my aunt asked him why he'd done it, he said, "It wasn't my fault. It was my willy."'

I laugh so much it makes my tummy ache.

Luke nudges me gently and says, 'It's nice to hear you laugh.'

We reach my house and I hesitate, unsure how to end things. I find my notepad. *Thanks for walking me home. Very gallant of you!*

When Luke smiles, a dimple creases his cheek. 'No probs. Any time.'

I glance up. Luke takes a step towards me, his expression unsure, then he stops, shakes his head with a rueful smile, and steps back again.

'Sleep well, Megan.'

I walk down the garden path, pausing on the doorstep. Was that . . . ? Was he going in for a kiss? No. Jasmine's wrong. She's so wrong.

I realise that Luke's waiting for me to get inside before he leaves. I pretend I can't find my keys, then wave them at him like a dork.

When I open the front door, a blast of sound hits me. The TV's turned up to full volume. Great. Mum's drunk.

In the lounge, she's draped across the sofa like a scruffy old blanket. The tang of wine is so strong I can almost taste it. Sure enough, there's an empty bottle on the floor. Her stilettos have been abandoned halfway across the room, like she just stepped out of them and flopped on to the sofa.

When she sees me, Mum reaches for the TV remote, but she's clumsy and it crashes to the floor. She huffs and tries again. I step in, retrieve it and press the mute button.

'Was that Luke out there?' she slurs. 'He your boyfriend now? About bloody time! I haven't seen him in ages. When you bringing him round?'

I shake my head.

'Why not? You embarrassed of me?'

I use the TV guide to write her a note: *Just a friend. It wasn't a date. Jasmine was there.*

She gets this nasty look on her face. 'Jasmine. Your new best buddy.'

I take a startled step back.

'Where you going? I'm talking to you. Am I too old for you to hang around with? Not cool enough?'

This is ridiculous! I think. *Why are you jealous? You're my mum, not my friend.*

'I've been sitting here on my own.' Her face falls and she says quietly, 'I used to have loads of friends.'

Used to. Before you had me. I'm sorry, Mum. Sorry I screwed it all up for you.

I storm towards the hallway.

'You know the worst thing about having a daughter who doesn't speak?' she screeches.

I pause at the door.

'There's no one to have a decent argument with.'

I slam it behind me.

'Megan!' she wails as I fly up the stairs. 'Megan, I'm sorry! I didn't mean it. Come back and gimme a cuddle.'

Upstairs, I chuck my pyjamas on, then throw myself on the bed.

She hates you. You ruined her life.

My eyes sting with unshed tears.

My phone buzzes. It's Jasmine:

What happened? Spill! Xxx

I frown. How does she know I argued with Mum? Then I realise she means Luke. I reply:

Nothing happened! And nothing's going to happen. We're just friends xxx

I'm getting tired of repeating this. But I'm less convinced now. There was something going on tonight. Could he . . . ? No, he couldn't, he really couldn't.

Jasmine texts:

How boring! I wanted juicy details! Xxx

I could make some up? Xxx

LOL! :) xxx

Several minutes later, Jasmine texts again:

I'm so sleepy. Night night xxx

I smile.

Night xxx

How did she do that? Without even trying, she's calmed me down, taken all the anger away. More effective than an hour-long session with Mr Harwell.

The TV rumbles beneath me. Some stupid show where celebrities pamper and preen their dogs and enter them in a kind of beauty competition. Eventually, Mum switches it off and I hear her stumbling and giggling up the stairs.

My door creaks open. I clamp my eyes shut.

'My beautiful girl,' she whispers. 'I'm sorry. I'm always messing up. I love you.'

She plants an awkward kiss on my forehead.

When I wake the next morning, I'm instantly alert, though I don't know what woke me. Then I hear Mum crashing around and swearing in the bathroom. It's 6 a.m. Not her favourite time. Not her usual wake-up time, either. She's early.

I get up. Luckily, Mum left the door unlocked. I find her in the bath, sprawled on her back like an upended beetle, with the collapsed shower curtain wrapped around her. She's still got her nightie on, though it's rucked up around her hips and I get a glimpse of silky black knickers before I look away.

Thanks, Mum. That's exactly what I want to see first thing in the morning!

'What you doing in here?' she groans.

I don't respond. Obviously.

'I was trying to turn the shower on, but I slipped and the stupid curtain came down. I'm all right. I can manage.'

I look at her. A whisper of mirth winds through me. I try to bat it down, but I can't help it. My giggle quickly turns into a full-blown laugh.

Mum starts to glare, but the corners of her mouth pull up and soon she's laughing too. 'I'm hopeless!' she gasps. 'Will you help me up?'

As I heave her to her feet, Mum clutches her head and groans. 'Ooof. I'm never drinking again.'

She sees my expression. 'Yeah, yeah. I know I always say that, but this time I mean it. I'm really not in the mood for work today. I feel like crap.'

I leave her and plod back to bed. When I emerge later, the scent of burnt sugar drifts through the house. I'm still full from last night, but follow my nose downstairs, where Mum is poking a knife into the toaster, muttering under her breath.

I grab the knife before she electrocutes herself, and set it down on the work surface. A waffle is gently steaming on a small plate, its corners a little blackened. Mum's used squeezy chocolate sauce to draw a smiley face on it. It's quite sweet, really. She must have dragged her hangover to the shop this morning to buy supplies.

Mum hands me the plate with pride and we sit at the table together, her clutching a giant mug of coffee. 'So, you and Jasmine are getting on well, then?'

I nod, cramming a piece of sticky waffle in my mouth.

'I know I was completely out of order last night. I'm glad you've found a new friend, after everything that happened with . . .'

I shake my head. We're not talking about that.

'OK, OK.' She holds up her hands in a gesture of peace. 'I'm just saying, I think it's really good for you to have a new friend.'

At school, we have a presentation about starting sixth form. We made our choices last term. I can't wait to start my Photography A-level. I can't believe I actually get to study something I love so much.

When I get home, I tip my shoebox of photos on to the bed. I flick through several shots, looking at them critically. One shows a single shaft of sunlight piercing through heavy clouds. Another is a blackbird perched in a tree, the oily sheen of its feathers glinting in the weak, early winter light. One of my favourites is an autumnal scene of ponies grazing in a clearing, their coppery coats in perfect harmony with the rust-coloured bracken and ochre leaves.

There are no photos of people. It's not really my thing. Grandpa was good at portraits. I drag out one of his massive albums and look through it. I laugh at a shot of Mum, standing in Grandpa's kitchen with a cheeky grin on her face. I'm behind her – a chubby toddler clutching a cake bowl, the mixture smeared across my mouth. I remember the TV was blaring in the background. It must've been a Sunday because the *EastEnders* omnibus was on.

I start to hum the theme tune. The sound starts off hoarse and rough, but then it smooths over like shiny, polished wood as my voice awakens.

Stop it!

I stop. I take a deep, shaky breath and wait for my heart to stop galloping.

In Grandpa's album, there's a picture of him kneeling beside his vegetable patch, trowel in hand, looking up at the camera. I can tell by the look in his eyes that it was Gran who took the photo. Grandpa's face, with its many shadowed wrinkles, always reminded me of tree bark. As a child, I longed to press my fingertips into the grooves to see if they were as scratchy as they looked.

I turn back to my own shots and compare them to Grandpa's. He used to tell me I had a talent. I hope he was right, especially now I'm signed up for this Photography A-level.

I spent weeks agonising over my sixth-form application. I could've opted to stay at safe, familiar Barcham Green. They don't do Photography, though, so I chose a scary new place, about twenty miles away, where no one knows about my problem. Mum said I shouldn't worry about it. I think she was hoping I'd be speaking by now.

Just the thought of September – of the new routine, the new people, the bus ride without Jasmine or Luke – makes me feel sick. I wonder if I'm going to regret this. I wonder how many other decisions in my life are going to be more complicated because I don't speak. I wonder if there will ever be an end to it.

CHAPTER THIRTEEN

When Jasmine and I arrive at the school bus stop the next morning, there's an atmosphere. I glance around to see what everyone's looking at. Josh and Ben are having a go at Callum. Even Jasmine stops talking to listen to them.

'Which one would you do? Come on. Choose.'

They're waving a dirty magazine in front of him and he's backing away, blushing. 'Ha! He can't do it!' Ben slaps the magazine with glee. 'I told you, mate. He's gay! You wanna be careful when you're getting changed. Don't want him checking out your nob.'

Josh puffs out his chest and yells, 'You'd better not be looking at me, queer-boy.'

Ben whoops and starts to dance around the pair, taunting them. 'He fancies you, man. That's what it is! Look how embarrassed he is!'

Callum's face is flaming. Tears are gathering in his eyes and his mouth puckers as he tries to hold them back.

I shift my weight from foot to foot. Poor Callum. This is horrible. But a tiny part of me – a cowardly, shameful part – is just relieved that it's not me.

In the afternoon, I see Mr Harwell. I'm expecting another half an hour of just sitting and breathing. Easy enough.

'How have you been this week, Megan?'

Mr Harwell smells of cherry yoghurt today. I wonder if his wife prepares a packed lunch for him.

'Anything you'd like to share?'

I shrug.

'Well, let's run through our exercises first, then I'd like to try a couple of new things with you, if that's OK?'

I frown. I'm not good with 'new things'. He talks me through this activity where I tense every part of my body, one at a time, then release them. I'm dubious at first, but by the end I do feel better. My limbs are more relaxed, my head almost too heavy for my neck.

'So how are things at home, Megan?'

My head snaps up and my muscles tighten again.

'I don't want you to say anything. I thought maybe I could ask you "yes" and "no" questions and you could just give me a thumbs-up or a thumbs-down. Would that work?'

I'm guessing I don't have much choice. I nod.

'You live with your mum. Is that right?'

Thumb up.

'And do you have any contact with your dad?'

Thumb down. I never wanted to, either, after what he did.

Mr Harwell's pen scratches across his notepad. 'So your grandpa occasionally came to parents' evenings instead of your mum?'

Thumb up. With a flush of shame, I remember Mum breezing in late one year, all done up like she was going out. As her heels clipped across the gym floor, all the other parents turned to stare.

'Were you close to your grandpa?'

Thumb up.

'And how is your relationship with your mum?'

I don't respond.

Mr Harwell shifts in his seat. It releases a gentle creak, like a sigh. 'Sorry. We need "yes" and "no" questions, don't we? Let's move on.' He turns to a new sheet in his notepad. 'One of the teachers told me that you've made friends with Jasmine Pearce. Are you getting on well?'

Thumb up. To my surprise, I even make a small murmur of agreement.

Careful.

I take a deep, shuddery breath.

'Good. That's really great, Megan.' A pause. 'It must be nice to have someone again.'

My heart stops. I know where this is going.

'I understand it's painful.'

You understand nothing!

I get up.

'It's OK, Megan.'

No, it's not. It's really not. And we're not discussing this. Ever.

My fingers scrunch up, the nails biting into my palms. But I barely feel it.

'Megan, please sit down. I'm just trying to help you.'

I didn't ask for your help!

My breaths are coming out in great, ragged gusts. My skin is burning, my fists clenching and unclenching.

'Megan, it's natural to feel guilty after we lose someone.'

Clenching. Unclenching.

'Perhaps also anger?'

Anger? You have no idea!

'Were you angry that you'd been left alone?'

I slap him across the cheek. Waves of hot pain throb through my fingers. I leave and run down the corridor.

You pushed me too far. Put that in your bloody notes. Too far.

The bell for break rings as I charge into the toilets, almost colliding with someone by the sinks. I swerve past her and dash into the nearest stall, slamming the lock into place and leaning against the door. My hand is sore and shaky. Did I really just do that? Did I really just slap Mr Harwell?

When I look up, I realise I'm not in my usual cubicle. There's unfamiliar graffiti and the toilet roll dispenser is broken. No! It's wrong. It's all wrong. I always use the same toilet. Always!

'Megan?' a quiet voice says. It's Grace. 'Are you all right?'

No. Clearly not.

'Has Sadie upset you?'

Sadie? This isn't about Sadie. Just because your life revolves around her!

Grace seems hesitant, but she says, 'I know she can go a bit far sometimes.'

I snort. *If you know that, why don't you have the guts to stand up to her?*

'I sometimes wish ... I don't know. We used to have fun, didn't we?' She giggles nervously.

I close my eyes. *Fun. Yes. Of course I remember. But you're Sadie's friend now. You can't have it both ways.*

I do miss Grace. I always liked her. She was so mild-natured – the only one in our group who could smooth out our petty arguments.

'Listen, Megan. We all feel bad about what happened. I just want you to know that you're not—'

Outside, the door opens and Sadie says, 'Who are you talking to?'

'N-no one.'

'Someone's in there.'

'It doesn't matter.'

'Whatever. Come on, I need you in the form room.'

'Why?'

'New girl just got a higher mark than Lindsay for some Drama thing. Lindsay's on the warpath.'

Jasmine's just trying to keep her head down. Why can't they leave her alone?

After they've gone, I wait a couple of seconds, then creep into the third cubicle from the left. My cubicle. The one that used to say SADIE IS A SLAG before someone scribbled it out with thick, black marker pen.

I pull down the seat and plonk myself on it, glaring at a hole that someone's tried to gouge in the door. The scent of bleach irritates my nose. My eyes stay fixed on that hole. It blurs and shimmers. I let one tear fall. And that's enough. The rest quickly follow.

A few minutes later, Jasmine comes in to look for me, knocking on each door as she calls out, 'Megan?'

Go away!

But she won't. 'I know it's you in there. I've looked everywhere else. You might as well let me in. If you don't, I'll climb over. Come on, Megan, let me in.'

I unlock the door with one hand, clutching the other to my chest, fingers curled inwards. Jasmine shuffles through the narrow gap. She takes a long look at my face, my reddened hand, the way I'm holding it, and her eyes widen. 'Oh my God, have you been in a fight? Who was it? Wait, let me guess. Sadie. That bitch! This isn't on, Megan. We need to stop this. I'm going to whatshisname, Finnigan. I'm going—'

I wave my good hand to stop her from talking. I mime slapping her. Jasmine frowns. 'OK. You slapped someone?'

I nod.

'Sadie?'

I shake my head. Why does this have to be so hard? Why can't I just open my mouth like a normal person, instead of playing this stupid game of charades? How long before Jasmine gets tired of trying to read my mind? How long before she gives up? Finds someone else to hang around with.

She won't stick around for long.

Jasmine grasps my shoulders. 'Megan,' she says seriously. 'Who did you hit?'

I turn around for my rucksack. It's not there! I must've left it in the stationery cupboard. For God's sake! I yank a piece of toilet paper off the roll. Jasmine looks through her bag and produces a pen. I write: *Mr Harwell.*

Her mouth flops open. 'Noooo! You hit a teacher? I mean, not like a proper teacher, but ... Why?'

It's too complicated to explain with gestures, too difficult to write down.

Jasmine thinks for a moment. 'We need to sort this out. You could be expelled or something. I think you should apologise to him.' She starts to unlock the door, but I drag her away, shaking my head. *I can't. I'm sorry I hit him, but I can't face him again.*

'You need to apologise. Before he reports you to Finnigan.'

She opens the door and tries to tug me out.

No! I don't want to. Leave me alone! Stop treating me like a child.

I grit my teeth and pull away from her. Argh! A voice would really come in handy now!

'Megan, don't look at me like that! What's the matter with you?'

What's the matter with me? *What's the matter with* you? *Since when do you tell me what to do? Do you think that, just because I can't speak, you can boss me around?*

Jasmine is standing in the doorway, half in and half out. I see the hurt in her eyes. I know I'm going to feel guilty for this later, but I can't stop myself. I push past her.

'Where are you going?' Jasmine demands.

When I don't stop to explain, she yells, 'Fine. Run away. But don't expect me to save you a seat in French.'

I rush towards the fire escape. I don't care if I set the alarm off. I have to get out! But my hand hovers over the lever. I rest my forehead against the cool door, pause, and think. Jasmine's right. I can't run away from this. I need to find Mr Harwell.

I walk as quickly as I can to the stationery cupboard, but he's not there. I grab my bag, hurrying towards Reception. What if he's telling Mr Finnigan right now? What's going to happen to me? I can't be expelled before I've taken my GCSEs!

Mr Harwell isn't at Reception. I rush out to the car park, scanning the rows of cars, but there's no one around. Where is he? I stand in the middle of the tarmac, paralysed. I literally have no idea what to do.

A breeze floats past and lifts the hair from my neck. It's scented with something sweet. Cherry blossom. There's a big tree in the corner of the car park, laden with delicate petals. I close my eyes and breathe it in. Deeply, like Mr Harwell taught me. I imagine everything is drifting away, like dandelion heads in the wind.

I open my eyes. I feel better. I can fix this. I've got his email address. I'm supposed to be in French now, but maybe I can sneak off to the library and send him a quick email to apologise.

The bell rings as soon as I step back inside. I march towards the library. I'm almost there when a crisp voice stops me: 'I don't think you'll find my French class in there, Megan Thomas.'

I stop dead. Turn to face Madame Girard.

'Shall I show you the way, as you seem to have forgotten?'

I nod sheepishly, then fall into step behind her. Madame Girard is stout, with ruddy cheeks and hair that looks constantly windswept. She wears a green gilet instead of a coat. As she strides down the corridors, I almost expect to see a couple of hunting dogs bounding after her.

In the classroom, Jasmine's sitting near the front, tapping her pen against a textbook in a rapid, nervous rhythm, her foot jiggling beneath the desk. She shoots a quick glance at the door, turning her head in a jerky movement. As soon as she sees me, her eyes flick away.

I slide into the seat next to Jasmine, searching her face, but she won't look at me. I try touching her arm, but she flinches like there's poison dripping from my fingers. *OK! No need to make me feel like a leper. Slight overreaction.*

Irritatingly, I've forgotten my French textbook, so I have to scoot closer to share Jasmine's. She doesn't acknowledge me. *Great. Thanks a lot. I love being ignored. It's not like I already feel invisible most of the time.*

Without preamble, Madame Girard launches into revision of French verbs. I do my best to focus, but my gaze is drawn to

Jasmine. I try to catch her eye. It works, but she instantly looks away.

Wait! I looked right at her! This is huge! I can usually only manage eye contact with Mum, and even then I feel awkward. Does this mean I might be getting better? Is it possible—?

You'll never change.

I jolt so much my chair scrapes across the floor.

Madame Girard glowers at me. '*Êtes-vous bien,* Megan?'

I nod and blush, leaning forward so I can pretend to study the textbook.

'Megan?' The school receptionist sticks her head around the door. ' Mr Finnigan would like to see you.'

The blood freezes in my veins. I get up and follow her to the head's office.

Mr Harwell is waiting inside. I peek up at his face. One of his cheeks is slightly flushed. I can't believe I did that. I shouldn't have lost it.

'Megan, Mr Harwell has reported that you assaulted him in your session today.'

Assaulted. Such a cruel word. A criminal word.

'This is absolutely unacceptable, Megan. Do you understand?'

I nod.

'We've spoken to your mother,' my stomach spasms, 'and have agreed two weeks of lunchtime detentions, starting tomorrow. Mr Harwell is prepared to continue working with you, provided you apologise and assure him that it won't happen again.'

I nod and point at a fancy fountain pen on Mr Finnigan's desk. He pushes it towards me and watches as I write my apology.

'I'm disappointed, Megan. Mr Harwell is an excellent, newly qualified psychologist who is more than capable of helping you. I suggest you start allowing him to do so.'

I nod. But I can't let him help me. I can't risk revealing the truth.

You need to keep this a secret, understand?

If I don't keep my mouth shut, people will find out what really happened to Hana at the ridge. They'll find out what a monster I am.

CHAPTER FOURTEEN

'I mean, seriously, what the hell, Megan? You hit your psychologist?'

Apparently.

'What will people think? That I didn't bring you up properly? I'm so embarrassed.'

I scrawl: *That's all you ever worry about – what people think. What about what I think? What about why I did it?*

'Well, go on then. Explain it to me. Why did you do it?'

I just stare at her.

'I thought so. God, I wish Gramps was here. He was the only one who could get through to you. I just don't understand you, Megan!'

I leave her desperately puffing on an e-cigarette and disappear to my room. I wonder whether to text Jasmine. I didn't see her at lunch – I hid in the library – and she wasn't on the bus home. I spent several panicky minutes convinced she was avoiding me, that I'd ruined everything, until I remembered she'd planned to stay and work on some Art coursework.

I write:

I'm sorry xxx

She makes me wait twenty minutes before replying.

It's OK. What happened? X

Two weeks of detention. Mum hit the roof :(Am hiding in my room xxx

A reply comes back a few minutes later:

Poor you. *Hugs* Want to come round for tea? Xxx

Meet her family? I don't know.

Mum's making mezze. They want to meet you xxx

I grin.

Will check with Mum xxx

Bring some of your pics if she says yes. I really want to see them! Xxx

Downstairs, Mum reads the note I've written, then looks long and hard at me. 'I should ground you,' she says.

You've never grounded me in your life!

'But I won't, because I want to watch *Pimp Your Pooch* while I eat, and I can't be dealing with you sighing all over it. Make sure you come home in a better mood.' She gives me a wry smile. 'Off you go! Before I change my mind!'

'Muuuum!' Jasmine yells as she bundles me through her front door.

I almost trip over a box of shoes. The hallway is long, narrow and dark, the carpet ripped a little at the edges. But it's brightened by a series of exotic paintings: elephants silhouetted against a savannah sunset, a landscape of paddy fields, scattered with figures wearing triangular hats.

A plug-in freshener is lacing the air with a floral smell. When I take a further step inside, another freshener bursts into life, spraying droplets of citrusy perfume on my arm.

Jasmine rolls her eyes. 'I told you she's into smells. She had those out before we'd even unpacked the kitchen.'

'Muuuum!' Jasmine hollers again. 'Megan's here.'

A woman emerges at the end of the corridor, holding her hands out as if they're covered in something sticky. 'Megan!' she half shrieks, half laughs, in a slightly accented voice. 'You're here! We finally get to meet you! Come in. Welcome. There's plenty of food.'

'There's *always* plenty of food,' Jasmine says, before whispering to me, 'I should've warned you: she's a feeder.

Hope you're hungry because she won't stop until you puke!'

Jasmine's mum rushes down the corridor. Her skin has the same rich tone as Jasmine's and her clothes are vibrant blues and oranges, like a kingfisher. A mass of grey-streaked curls are swept back into a ponytail, and her slightly crooked teeth peep out behind a smile so wide it stretches across most of her face.

'I'm Eleni, Megan. It's wonderful to meet you.' She sweeps me into a hug and I'm surrounded by the scent of green tea, lavender and musky incense. 'Arthur and I are thrilled that Jas has made a friend so soon. *Apanagía mou,* I'm sorry, I've just got oil on your back. I'm making *dolmádes* and I'm covered in the stuff. Take your coat off and I'll try to rinse it. Your mother's not going to be pleased with me. What an awful first impression! *Signómi. Éla,* come through.'

Eleni continues to talk as she herds me into a small kitchen. Her English is fluent, though she peppers it with Greek, tossed in like chunks of feta in a salad.

The kitchen smells incredible. Its counters are strewn with mess: a Greek yoghurt pot; sprigs of mint; onion and garlic skins; deflated lemon halves.

'I'm making a feast!' Eleni announces, throwing her hands in the air.

A small head pokes round the door. Jasmine looks up and a smile breaks across her face. 'Lily *mou*! This is my friend, Megan.'

Lily nods shyly, casting a furtive glance in my direction. 'Hello,' she whispers.

I nod and try to smile back.

Don't.

I blush and instantly look down.

'I'm Lily.' She holds out a hand that's covered with dried glue and pieces of glitter. 'I've been making a birthday card.'

I shake her hand. *I'm Megan. I wish I could tell you my name.*

Don't say anything.

I jump a little, then whip my hand away from Lily's before she notices how much it's trembling. Lily comes further into the kitchen and swipes a golden ball off a dish on the counter. Compared with her sister, her skin is paler, her hair not as dark and glossy, more of a light brown. She shares those big, beautiful eyes though, and they rove greedily across all the food.

Jasmine points at the round thing Lily is nibbling. 'That's a falafel. Have you had one before?'

I shake my head.

'They're ace. Technically not Greek, but we still love 'em! Try one.'

She picks one up and raises it to my mouth, which drops open in surprise. The brush of Jasmine's fingers against my lips sends tingles through me. I try to look normal and chew, even though there's no saliva left. Jasmine turns away and I manage to swallow. It's delicious – warm, crispy and herby.

'These,' Jasmine tugs my arm, gesturing at some knobbly,

sausage-like patties, 'are *kofte*. Lamb. Good job you're not a veggie. Lily is, but she doesn't know what she's missing out on.'

Lily sticks her tongue out. It's covered with mushed-up brown stuff.

'It's ready!' Eleni announces. 'Lily, go and fetch Dad, will you?'

Lily nods, then turns and scampers up the stairs.

Jasmine and I grab a couple of dishes and carry them to the dining table, which is set in the corner of a large living room. Two sofas are buried under mounds of precariously stacked boxes and bulging bin bags. There's a rolled rug propped against the window, a bag of coat hangers on the table and the TV has been plonked in the middle of the floor with a purple toilet air freshener perched on top of it.

Eleni apologises again. '*Signómi,* sorry, sorry,' she breathes. 'What a tip. We really need to start moving this stuff. What must you think of us?'

It's OK. You should see our place.

As Jasmine and Eleni return to the kitchen for more food, I settle at the table and my attention flits from dish to tantalising dish.

Heavy footsteps plod down the stairs. Seconds later, Jasmine's dad appears. He's so tall his grey, tousled hair almost touches the top of the doorframe. Bags hang like rainclouds beneath his eyes, which are a sharp, light blue.

'Hello, I'm Arthur. You must be Megan. Nice to meet you.'

He holds out a hand, which I shake, surprised by his firm grip. 'Where do you live, Megan?'

Silence descends, as thick as clotted cream. *Jasmine, where are you?* Her dad is frowning at me, I can feel it.

He doesn't know what Jasmine sees in you.

'Da-ad,' Jasmine groans as she steps into the room. 'I told you about Megan. Don't you ever listen to me?'

'Oh. I . . . er. Of course you did. I remember now. Sorry, Megan.'

'So embarrassing,' Jasmine mumbles.

True to Jasmine's warning, Eleni is a 'feeder', and by the time the mezze is over, I'm so full, I can't imagine being hungry ever again. My ribs ache and my head is woozy from too much laughter.

The meal was hilarious, raucous, exciting. The conversation, driven by Jasmine and Eleni, darted from subject to subject so fast I could barely keep up. Every now and then, little Lily piped up with something, her sweet voice cutting through her mother and sister's chatter. Arthur was content to lean back in his chair and just watch.

'Urgh. I feel disgusting,' Jasmine complains, clutching her stomach. 'I'm too full to move.'

Eleni smiles. 'You'll have to move some time. You can't sleep here.'

'I could,' counters Jasmine. 'If you leave this all out, I might wake up in the night and fancy a midnight snack.'

'Yes, there's too much left. Are you sure you can't manage any more, Megan?'

I shake my head. I wish I could. I'm so glad I tried it. I've never tasted anything like it before. It was gorgeous. Every mouthful. From the delicately spiced *kofte* to the garlicky hummus and the refreshing, crisp Greek salad.

'Would you like to take some home for your mum, Megan?' Eleni asks.

Mum probably had a rubbery ready meal for dinner. I nod and Eleni promises to package a few things up.

'Is it OK if Megan stays for a bit?' Jasmine asks.

Arthur agrees.

I try to smile at Eleni as we leave, to thank her for the meal, but I'm not sure she sees me. I should write her a note or something.

Upstairs, I settle on Jasmine's bed. My eyes wander around her room. There's a cup of tea-dredges on the floor and a plate with breadcrumbs on. Her underwear drawer is open, with a pair of knickers and a bra spilling over the edge. The light blue walls are decorated with posters of Grace Kelly and Audrey Hepburn.

Jasmine sees me looking. 'Horrible colour, isn't it? I can't wait to redecorate.'

I find a notepad in my bag and write: *I was looking at the posters.*

'Oh, them! Aren't they glamorous?'

I nod.

'Did you bring the photos?'

I pull Grandpa's camera and a pile of photos from my rucksack. I pass the Canon to Jasmine. Sensing its significance, she holds it carefully. I write: *It was my grandpa's.*

Jasmine runs her fingers over the casing. Her nails are smooth and shiny, the tips white and clean, unlike my bitten, ragged stumps. 'It's beautiful,' she murmurs. 'Can I see the photos?'

I nod and grab a handful for her to flick through. I really should put them in an album, organise them somehow. I watch as a series of shots flash through Jasmine's hands – birds, trees, leaves, rivers, the moor, the forest, Brookby.

'Wow, Megan. These are good! I mean, really good! You're so talented. I'd happily stick one of these up on my wall.'

Really? You think I'm good?

I write: *Take one.*

Jasmine shakes her head. 'I wasn't hinting. They're yours. You should keep them.'

I point to my message, insisting.

'OK, thanks.'

Jasmine flashes that glorious smile and starts to pick through them, inspecting each photo. She settles on a close-up of dew-drops glistening on spears of grass.

'Jasmine, time for Megan to go,' Eleni shouts up the stairs. 'Don't you have French homework?'

Jasmine scowls. 'I was hoping she'd forgotten.' She picks up her textbook and slams it on the desk. Something falls out of the pages. A note with her name on.

Jasmine stares at it in silence for a few moments, then says in a low voice: 'You read it.'

I pick the note up and unfold it. It's written in angular block capitals, with each word scratched deep into the paper, as if whoever wrote it was pouring all their anger into every stroke of the pen. My skin ices over.

YOU MAKE ME SICK. YOU'RE A STUPID BITCH IF YOU THINK ANYONE LIKES YOU.

CHAPTER FIFTEEN

I glance up at Jasmine, my mouth stupidly frozen in a small 'o'. She won't meet my eyes. 'I've had a couple since I arrived. I thought I was leaving stuff like this behind,' her voice cracks, 'but it just follows me!'

What did the others say? I write on the back of some revision notes.

Jasmine still won't look at me. 'Horrible stuff.'

Like?

'"Why would Owen fancy a minger like you?" Stuff like that. It must be the same person who messed with Owen's graffiti.'

Who? I scribble.

'Some of the girls from my old school know people here. They might have put them up to it. Or – I don't know – Sadie, maybe?'

Maybe. Or it could be Lindsay. What was it Sadie said the other day? Lindsay was on the warpath. I should've warned Jasmine.

'Owen told me that he and Sadie were an item over the summer. She's probably pissed off that I'm friends with you, and that I'm seeing Owen.'

So are you 'seeing' Owen?

Jasmine blushes a little. 'I dunno. I bumped into him at the weekend, after I left yours. I was feeling a bit ... you know, wobbly, and he was nice to me. Took my mind off it.'

I grit my teeth. I bet he did.

'Listen, about Friday night. He said he wasn't thinking.'

That's bull. He knew exactly what he was doing. He was trying to get a reaction out of me.

I don't want to argue so I point to the vicious note and raise my eyebrows.

Jasmine sighs. 'I don't know what to do about them. Mum will go mental if I tell her.'

I read the message again. A shiver snakes across my skin. Shouldn't we tell someone? I'm afraid for her. What if this person is dangerous?

We're getting close to our first exams now. Every lesson at school is filled with revision or practice papers. We spend every spare minute studying. Despite this, I'm still managing to see Mr Harwell once or twice a week. After the slap, it was as awkward as I'd imagined. He seemed a bit embarrassed that he'd had to report me.

The first two weeks of exams pass in a blur of sleepless nights and information overload. We have a break for May half-term, but we'll have to spend most of it cramming.

On Tuesday, I head to Jasmine's for English revision.

'This is so boooring!' she says with a yawn, stretching back on her bed and kicking her copy of *Wuthering Heights* to the floor.

I lie down too, propping my head in my hand. Jasmine's eyes are closed. Even without mascara, her lashes are jet black and really thick. Her smooth, rose-coloured lips are moist and slightly parted, her breaths coming out soft and slow.

I want to kiss her.

I'm sorry ... *what*?

What the hell was that? Where did it even come from?

'Isn't Cathy the most annoying character ever?'

What? Who?

Jasmine opens her eyes. 'Why are you so red?'

I'm not. Stop staring at me! You're making it worse!

'Seriously, Megan, you look like you're about to explode. Want me to open a window?'

I nod.

She gets up and walks across the room.

Stop looking at her bum, Megan! What's wrong with you?

'I was just saying, Cathy's such a whiney cow.'

I wanted to kiss her. Is that normal? Do other girls have random impulses to kiss their best friends?

'Megan? Hello? What are you thinking about? It's definitely not Cathy. Something far more interesting.' Jasmine sits cross-legged on the bed and taps my knee. I stare at the spot she's just touched.

'C'mon, what's going on? You look like a beetroot!'

Great. I look like a big, sweaty beetroot. That's attractive. But why do I care if I look attractive? Did I ever care how I looked for Hana? What does this mean?

Jasmine pouts. 'Aren't you going to tell me?'

Tell you? Absolutely not! And stop pouting. It's distracting.

She grins. 'You know you want to. Go on!'

I don't respond.

Jasmine frowns, thinks for a moment, then whisks the book off the floor, suddenly business-like. 'Well, we'd better get back to this then.'

She starts to find her page, but I don't move. I can't just sit here and read a stupid book like nothing's happened!

Jasmine snaps her book shut. 'You're seriously making me paranoid, Megan. Did I do something? Does my breath smell?'

I shake my head, grab some paper and write: *Sorry. Have to go. Not feeling so great.*

Jasmine's irritation is swept away by concern and she presses her hand to my forehead. My skin flares up again, even worse than before.

'You poor thing. You're boiling! Hang on, I'll get my stuff and walk you back.'

I'll be fine, I write. *Honestly*. I stand up.

Jasmine stands too. 'There's no way you're going on your own. I'm coming.'

One look at her expression and I know I won't be able to put her off.

Outside, I walk quickly, gulping the cool air, which soothes my burning skin. I'm vaguely aware that Jasmine is talking about some kid in her Science class who thinks he can beat the multiple choice tests by following a pattern in the answers.

That's not the first time I've wanted to kiss Jasmine. How could I have forgotten? That night at the ridge. I suppose it just got lost amongst all the Hana stuff. Would I have made a move if I hadn't realised where we were? What would she have done? Pushed me away, probably. Laughed at me. This isn't happening!

'All right?' someone grunts behind us. We stop. It's Owen. Great. Exactly who I want to see right now.

'Hi!' Jasmine says, with a dazzling smile.

'Where you going?'

Jasmine hesitates. 'I'm just walking Megan home.'

He puts his hand on her hip. On her hip! Ergh. 'You want a revision break?' he growls softly.

I shudder. I assume it won't be their first 'revision break'.

Jasmine is lost in Owen. It's like she's forgotten I'm even here. 'OK,' she breathes.

She wrenches herself away to look at me. 'You'll be all right?' She tries to make it sound like a question, though we both know it's more of a statement.

I nod, then turn and stride away. I can't believe her! One minute she's all worried about me, then she dumps me the second someone more interesting comes along. She's just like Hana.

Jasmine texts me later to ask if I got back OK. I ignore her. I need some space. I can't cope with this and exams. It's too much.

I lie in bed, but my body's humming with restless energy. There's no way I'll be able to sleep. By eleven, I've had enough. I get up, poke my head around Mum's door to check she's asleep, then sneak out.

I've done this a couple of times before. Just wandered around the village at night. I like that there aren't many people around. I don't know where I'm going, but that's OK. I don't need to know.

I end up at Jasmine's house. How did that happen? I pick at some flaky paint on her fence, wondering what I'm doing. I'm still angry with her for ditching me, but I really want to see her. Should I text, tell her I'm outside? No. That's too weird. Who just turns up on their friend's doorstep in the middle of the night? I wind a strand of hair around my finger, tighter and tighter, cutting off the circulation. Was Hana right about me being clingy? I should go.

I head home, my footsteps heavy.

I'm groggy and grumpy the next morning. I stare at a crack in the ceiling, trying to sort through my thoughts, but I'm not getting very far. Then Jasmine texts:

Megan, I got another note. Can you come round? Xxx

Why did this have to happen now? What do I do? I can't just abandon her. Well, I could. She abandoned me yesterday. No, that's cruel.

Another text arrives:

I'm freaking out. I need you! Xxx

I fling back my duvet and rush to find some clothes.

As I cycle to Jasmine's, I stress about how I'm going to act around her. Everything's changed. I don't want to be all awkward. I just wish I had more time to think this through!

As soon as Jasmine answers the door, I'm blushing and making even less eye contact than usual. Thank God I can't speak, or I'd be stammering and gibbering like an idiot.

Jasmine doesn't seem to notice, though. She drags me up to her room, where the note is lying on her bed. 'Someone pushed it through the front door!' she whispers. 'What if Mum or Dad had read it?'

I take a look.

YOU DISGUST ME. YOU DON'T DESERVE ANY FRIENDS.

This is sick! What kind of twisted, messed-up person would do this? I grab a pen and scribble all over the words, again and again, digging into the paper until it starts to tear. When I look up, Jasmine is watching me, wide-eyed. I breathe heavily through my nose, try to reign myself in before I completely lose it.

'What do we do?' she whimpers.

I fetch my notepad and write: *I don't know. I'm sorry.*

'If I tell Mum, she'll want to take me away again. She'll cancel my sixth-form place. I want to stay, Megan!'

I stare at Jasmine in horror. *No! You can't leave. Please!*

Jasmine and I spend the rest of half-term revising together. She's pretty jumpy, and I can tell she's not sleeping well. She's definitely struggling to focus. I try to help, but I'm really worried about how she's going to manage with exams.

Although I'm trying to be a good friend, I make an effort to not stare at her too much, not get too close or touch her unless I need to. Little things that used to mean nothing, like holding her hand, mean everything now. Whatever this is, Jasmine can't ever find out how I feel. There's no going back from something like that. It would ruin our friendship.

That's what you do, isn't it? Ruin friendships.

Back at school, Mr Harwell is all invigorated after his holiday and ready to try new things. 'Right, Megan,' he says with a clap. 'We're going to try a bit of humming today.'

I raise an eyebrow. Humming's OK. If I'm on my own. Not in front of others.

'Now, just give it a chance before you make up your mind. I've brought some CDs for you to look through. No mocking my bad taste! Why don't you pick one?'

I flick through the pile he's left on the desk. Some of his choices are seriously questionable, but there are a couple I wouldn't mind listening to.

Mr Harwell puts the CD in the player and lets me choose the track. 'Bitter Sweet Symphony' by The Verve. He closes his eyes – he knows it helps if he's not watching me – and starts to hum. He's completely out of tune. I stifle a giggle. Mr Harwell opens his eyes and gives me a look that tells me to take it seriously.

I nod, take one of those deep breaths we've practised, and focus on the music. I really do like this song. I feel the melody pulse through me, sing the lyrics in my mind. A few moments later, I start to make the smallest of sounds at the back of my throat.

The song finishes. Mr Harwell looks pretty pleased. 'Let's try it without music this time.'

Keep quiet.

I flinch.

Mr Harwell nods sympathetically. 'It's OK, Megan. You're safe here.'

I trust him, so I try to do it.

Silence. After a few minutes, Mr Harwell breaks it. 'There's no one to hear you except me.'

Another silence. He lets this one stretch out even longer.

'If you'd like to try something else today, Megan, we can move on and come back to this next week.'

I shake my head. I want to do it.

I swallow heavily, then close my eyes as one of Jasmine's favourite songs plays in my mind. It's from a West End musical. I'm not sure which one, but it's a beautiful, haunting love song. As soon as she played it to me, I loved it. It makes me smile to think that most teenagers are jumping around their rooms to boy-band pop while Jasmine is blasting out ballads from some bloke called Lloyd Webber.

I imagine I'm in her room. Jasmine's singing along lightly, almost under her breath. I hum the first few bars with her. The sound scratches and scrapes its way out, but it's there. It's really there!

I give up about halfway through the song. I've had enough. Mr Harwell still says he's proud of me. I'm proud of myself. I feel like we're loosening the clamp around my voice box, one tiny notch at a time.

You'll never talk again.

I should've known better. I'll never speak again. And, after what I did, I probably don't deserve to.

I try to get some revision done after school, but it's impossible. The sun is streaming through my bedroom window. I just need to be outside.

Minutes later, I'm on my bike, Grandpa's camera bumping gently against my hip.

I ride out to Stonylea Hill. Hana and I used to have

competitions to see who could get the furthest before giving up and pushing to the top. I usually won. Not because I was the fittest. I was just so stubborn. Once we were at the peak, the real fun began and we'd fly down the other side, wind whipping the hair off our sweat-soaked backs.

When I reach the top, I practically fall off my bike and drop into some leaf mulch by the side of the road. I lie on my back, gasping as I watch the leaves above tremble and twitch like butterfly wings. A woodpecker chips away at a tree somewhere behind me, and the call of a starling sounds out through the forest. I remain like this, listening, until my breaths start to even out.

Leaning my bike against a fence, I enter the forest. I stick to the main path for a while, then veer off to the left, down my own trail. My shoes crunch and rustle over fir cones and dry leaves. I disturb a deer that was crossing the path before me. Its ears flick back and forth, nostrils flaring, before it bounds off into the trees.

I reach my fallen oak. There's a beautiful curve to the trunk that's just perfect to sit in, as though it's been carved just for me. This is my most perfect, private place.

A beetle waddles across the bark beside me. It's jet black with a blue sheen. I pull out Grandpa's camera and focus on it. I take a couple of shots, following its progress to the ground.

I get off the tree and crouch down so I can take some close ups. But my lens catches something else behind the beetle. I pause. The camera falls from my frozen fingers and thunks into a pile of leaves.

Beneath the tree trunk, there's a hollow. Hana and I used to leave messages for each other here. There's something in that hollow now. Something white.

Oh. My. God.

I checked here. I know I did. After she … after it happened, I came here. But there's definitely something here now. I feel cold, then hot, then sick.

With clumsy hands, I reach for it. It's an envelope, wrapped in a sandwich bag. I peel off the wet bag, careful not to let it drip on the paper. My name dances across the front in her messy scrawl. I bite my lip to stifle a cry.

I stand on weak legs and lean against the tree trunk. I trace the letters with my fingertip, trying to imagine what she was thinking when she wrote it. My nail slips under the envelope flap. I hesitate. Do I really want to know?

A twig breaks. I jump and shove the letter in my jacket pocket. When I look up, Rob – Sadie's boyfriend – is standing in front of me, his absurdly chiselled jaw hanging open.

To my horror, Josh, Lindsay and Grace appear behind him, followed by Sadie, who looks disgusted as she staggers through the mud in a pair of heels.

This isn't happening. This is *my* place. And I need to read that letter. In private.

Before Rob can say anything, I leap up, stumble over the oak, and charge into the forest.

I'm off the main path. It's overgrown. Wild. I dodge through trees, leap over roots and rocks. Brambles and thorns snag my hair and thin branches whip across my face. Are they following me? I don't know. Can't hear anything but the fast thud of my heartbeat.

After a few minutes, I stop.

The letter. I have to read it now. I reach into my pocket.

It's gone.

CHAPTER SIXTEEN

No! The letter must've fallen out of my jacket. I've got to get it back. I pivot round and retrace my steps. Please let me find it before I reach my tree. Please don't make me go back. My eyes dart around, searching for a flash of white amongst the dry leaves and dirt.

But there's nothing. When I emerge in the clearing, my forehead damp with sweat and my hair all over the place, Lindsay smirks, places a hand on her hip and shouts, 'Look who it is, Sadie.'

Sadie glances up. She wraps her slender arms around Rob's waist. 'Hi, Megan.' Her voice drips with syrup. 'Have you come out to play with us?'

I don't respond. The letter is on my side of the fallen oak, in the shadows just beneath it. I don't think they can see it. My heart is pumping too fast.

Sadie says, 'No offence, but I don't think you're Rob's type.'

Lindsay throws back her head and laughs. Grace just blushes and looks down at her trainers.

'What's your problem?' Sadie snaps.

Grace's eyes widen. 'Nothing!' She lets out a fake laugh. 'But it's boring here. Let's go somewhere else.'

'What's wrong with here? I like it here.'

'But Megan's here,' Grace murmurs, her head tilted down.

Sadie smiles and her lip gloss glistens, soft and sticky as strawberry jam. 'I thought Megan was just leaving.'

I take a step towards her. Towards the letter.

'Have you forgotten something?' she asks with fake, mocking concern.

My eyes flit to the envelope. Stupid! Sadie's gaze follows. She leans over the tree trunk so she can see what I'm looking at. I start to move, but she pounces, snatching it up and scrunching it in her fist. A choking sound falls out of my mouth and I stretch out my arm.

Shut up!

Sadie waves it before me, her eyes alight. Cruel. 'Is this yours, Megan? It's got your name on it. Do you want it back?'

I nod once, my expression pleading.

'All you have to do is ask,' she says in a singsong voice.

I glare at the ground, my blood boiling.

Sadie draws her voice out, relishing each sound. 'Just ... one ... word.'

Enough! A coil of rage winds through me. With a raw cry, I grab Sadie's arm and yank her forward, slamming her hips into the tree, leaving her doubled over it. She shrieks, thrusts her arm back and shoves the letter at Rob, who takes it and stares at it dumbly.

'Bitch!' Sadie yells, brushing down her jeans. 'You're not ever having that letter back now.'

I shake my head. I need that letter. How can she not realise how important it is? I look up, letting her see how close I am to tears.

But Sadie just shakes her head. 'No. It's mine.'

What can I do? Short of wrestling them all to the ground, there's nothing. I had it in my hands and now I've lost it. I blink and a tear spills over my eyelid and trails down my cheek.

Rob is still staring at the letter, turning it over and over in his hands. 'Let's give it back, Sades,' he grunts.

Sadie rolls her eyes. 'It's just a stupid letter.'

It's not a stupid letter. You have no idea what it is, what it means.

Should I tell her who it's from? But what if she opens it? Reads it out in front of everyone so they can all laugh at me?

No one says anything. Sadie stares at Lindsay, but Lindsay looks away, nibbling one of her nails.

Sadie sighs. 'All right, Megan. I'll give it back.' She takes it from Rob and holds it out. I gasp and reach for it, but Sadie whips it away. 'When you stop hanging around with Jasmine.'

What? No. You can't ask me to do that. You can't take her away from me!

Sadie arches an eyebrow. 'I'll give her a second chance. I'm nice like that. You know you're just dragging her down. If she hangs around with us, she'll be popular, have loads of friends. Don't be selfish. She'd be much happier with us.'

How can I choose? How can she ask me to do that? Those are the last words that Hana ever wrote to me. I have to read them. I need to know what she was thinking. All this time, it's been tormenting me, eating me up, and now I have a chance to get inside her head.

But Jasmine. I can't give up on Jasmine. Hana's gone. She's ... she's gone. I can't change that. But I can protect Jasmine from Sadie, who'll probably just use her, then turn on her when it suits her. If Jasmine's right about Sadie sending the notes, I have to do everything I can to keep Sadie away from her.

I shake my head and back away.

Sadie shrugs. 'Fair enough. I gave you the choice. Now get lost, Megan.'

I walk away slowly. It takes everything I've got to hold myself together until I'm a safe distance away, then I slam my palm against a tree. It hurts, but – in a weird way – feels kind of good. With my face pressed against the bark, I sob into it, wrapping my arms around the trunk like it's a person, clinging to it to stop myself from sinking to the ground.

When I'm done, I stand up straight, brushing my cheeks with fierce strokes. I don't know how I'm going to do it, but I'll get that letter back from Sadie. I *will* get it back.

I walk along the road to collect my bike, then I ride home

quickly, taking my frustration out on the pedals. By the time I arrive, I'm a little dizzy, and shaking so much I struggle to get the key in the lock.

Mum comes to the door, takes one look at me, plucks a leaf from my hair and says, 'What the hell happened to you?'

I nudge past her to get inside.

'Megan!' Mum calls after me.

I put my bike in the utility room, scattering crumbs of mud across the floor. I stare at each dry piece of dirt, trying to count them all, trying to steady myself. But there are too many. My head starts spinning. I need to clean them up.

Mum stands in the doorway, folding her hands across her chest. 'What happened?'

I shake my head. *I can't.*

Mum follows me to the kitchen. She breathes in slowly through her mouth, drawing on an imaginary cigarette. 'Can you write it down?'

No. I'm sorry, Mum. You wouldn't understand.

I grab a dishcloth and start to clean the work surface. It's filthy.

'Can you leave that, please?'

No. It's gross.

'Come on, Megan. I'm your mum, for God's sake.'

I scrub at a soup stain on the cooker, my hand moving in rapid, angry swipes.

'I never know what you're thinking.' Mum's working herself up. Her eyes are red, her mouth scrunching as she tries to hold back tears. 'I want to make it better, but I don't know how.'

You can't, Mum. No one can.

She studies me for a moment, desperately searching my face for . . . I don't know what. Then the tears overflow and she yells, 'God! I'm not a mind reader, Megan. I wish you'd just talk to me!'

My mouth drops. She realises her mistake in an instant. I think she'd like to take her words back. But they hang in the air, dangling like twisted toys from a child's mobile.

I slam down the dishcloth, flicking dirty water over both of us. *This isn't a choice. Do you think I do it just to spite you?*

I stomp up to my room. How dare she? Mum has no idea.

I pause. Sigh. She has no idea because I haven't told her. She has a point. How is she supposed to know how I'm feeling? I know it's been hard for her too. Mum didn't want a baby when she was sixteen. She wanted to be out clubbing with her mates. She wanted to do her A-levels. She didn't want to be judged by every middle-class snob in the village. But I ruined everything.

You always do.

I wish I could call Hana. I wish I still had the letter. I imagine what it might have said, rewrite it a thousand times in my mind. It kills me that I had it in my hands and now I've lost it.

As soon as Jasmine and I arrive at the bus stop the next day, Sadie peels away from her crowd and heads towards us. My eyes flick to her massive handbag. I wonder if the letter is in there. How am I going to get it back? She's not exactly going to wander off and leave her bag alone. What if she just chucked the letter away last night? My throat thickens.

Sadie ignores me and goes straight for Jasmine. 'Your mate attacked me in the woods last night,' she announces.

Jasmine looks at me uncertainly. I shake my head, struggling to swallow.

'I'm telling you, she's unstable. I've got two massive bruises on my thighs and my jeans are ruined. You want to watch out. She's dangerous.'

Jasmine looks away. 'Seriously, Sadie. I'm not interested.'

Sadie thrusts her face into Jasmine's and hisses, 'Well, don't come running to me when you realise what a psycho she is. And tell *her*,' she barely looks at me, 'that if she ever touches me again, I'll slap her so hard her ugly nose will straighten.'

'What happened last night?' Jasmine asks softly, after Sadie has flounced back to her friends.

I can't tell her everything. She'll feel bad if she finds out I lost Hana's last letter because of her. I scribble: *She found me in the woods last night and took something from me. I tried to get it back.*

Jasmine stiffens. 'Were you writing to Hana again? I thought we talked about you not doing that.'

I glare at the ground. *Just because you think I should do something doesn't mean I have to do it.* I take a deep breath. It's OK. It's better she thinks that than knows the truth.

Jasmine looks like she's going to say something more, but the bus arrives, so she lets it drop.

Luke isn't waiting for us on the bus today. When Jasmine asks Simon why, he looks out the window for a moment, starts picking at some loose stitching in the back of Jasmine's seat, then finally says, 'He's off sick.'

'Oh no!' Jasmine replies. 'What's up with him?'

Simon blushes and mumbles something.

Jasmine leans closer. 'What did you say?'

Simon looks straight at her. 'Promise you won't tell?'

Jasmine and I exchange a glance. 'Okaaaay,' she agrees.

'He had a fight with Dad, then he broke a mirror, then he went out and didn't come back all night. Sometimes he just gets really mad, and he can't calm down.'

I frown. That doesn't sound like Luke. But I know he finds things tough where his dad is concerned. I hope he's OK. Maybe I should text him?

I have to clear my head and concentrate on a Maths exam in the morning, but I poke a note through a slit in Sadie's locker at lunchtime, asking her to return the letter. It's completely pointless. I know it is. I just need to do something. I try to reach the Sadie I used to know, the Sadie I liked and trusted. I remind her that, if our friendship meant anything, she'd give it back. I loiter round the corner, waiting, then watch helplessly as she glances at it, rolls her eyes, and screws it into a ball. I guess the Sadie I used to know is gone for ever.

Jasmine tries to cheer me up on the way to the bus after school. She tells me about the time she got in a pickle with her PE kit, forgot to put her knickers on, and spent the whole basketball lesson trying to shoot without jumping, in case someone saw up her shorts. I smile vaguely, but she can tell I'm distracted.

On the walk home, I can't really keep up with what Jasmine's saying. Something about a play she wants to see in London. Maybe if I can get hold of Sadie when she's not with the others, I can explain that the letter is from Hana, that I really need to read it. She must understand!

Jasmine drops me off at home and I rush inside to write Sadie another note. She can't just walk all over me because I don't have a voice to answer back. She's not getting away with this. That letter is mine!

My heart flips as I head up the path towards Sadie's front door. It's been a long time since I've been here. I remember having water fights in the front garden, her mum smiling at our shrieks as she washed her car in the drive. I glance up at the window we broke during a game of rounders. We had to save up our pocket money for weeks to replace it. And there's the spot we buried her hamster, Hugo, beneath the rose bush, along with a poem Sadie wrote for him.

The door swings open. Crap. Lindsay and Grace are with her. They've all changed out of their school uniforms, sorted their hair, and reapplied lipstick.

Grace delicately sidesteps me. When I catch her eyes, they seem to say: 'What are you doing here? Are you mad?'

Lindsay thuds her shoulder into mine. 'Where's your lesbo friend? Don't you need her to talk for you?'

Sadie's mouth puckers. She doesn't break her stride. 'I told you, you're not having it back. You can't now, anyway. I burnt it.'

What? No. You can't have. Surely even you wouldn't . . .

This is what happens to people like you. You brought this on yourself.

Sadie walks straight past, leaving me standing in the middle of her lawn, blinking tears away and trying to gather the strength to leave.

How could she? I can't believe it. My last link to Hana.

I've lost her all over again.

CHAPTER SEVENTEEN

My sessions with Mr Harwell are irregular at the moment, because of the exam timetable, but I think he's trying to fit more in before I finish at Barcham Green. He seems to be on some kind of personal mission to get me talking before sixth form. Like that's going to happen. I'm touched that he's still trying, though.

'How are you, Megan?' he asks.

Fed up of exam stress.

He leans forward. 'Listen. As much as I'd like to, I won't be working with you when you start college, so I think this will be our last session.'

Oh, really? OK.

'I'm going to push you a little today, Megan, but I think you can handle it.'

You mean you hope I won't hit you again?

'Now, I know there are some things you don't want to revisit.'

No. We're not going there.

'You've spent a long time building up a dam in your mind to hold all these memories, these emotions back. And I'm not suggesting that we try to access them all at once. That would be too much. But perhaps we can remove a tiny piece of the dam today. And you could work on taking a few more down over the summer?'

No.

But he's not giving in. 'Can you write down something you remember about Hana's death? Just a little detail.'

I can't.

'I want you to try, Megan. In fact, we're not leaving this room until you do.'

Mr Harwell sits back, folds his arms and watches me.

There's a wave of grief and guilt behind the dam. He really doesn't want me to unleash it.

We sit in silence for about ten minutes before I sigh, grab a pen and scribble: *I was really mad with Hana.*

The barricade groans, threatens to break, but I hold everything back. If I don't, I'll go mad.

We had a fight, I write. *I thought she was acting like a bitch. And I hate that she died knowing that.*

I swallow back my tears and look up at him. Mr Harwell doesn't speak for a long time, while he considers what to say. 'There are always things you could've said or done differently, Megan. Everyone has regrets after we lose someone. It's a common feeling, along with guilt, so I don't want you to feel alone in that. You and Hana had known each other for a long time, and I'm guessing you'd had other arguments?'

I nod.

'But your friendship always survived them. Your feelings of anger towards Hana were temporary. What lay beneath those feelings – the solid base of your friendship – didn't and hasn't changed. Would you say that's fair?'

I think about it. I suppose so. Kind of. Maybe.

Mr Harwell smiles, says, 'Thank you for sharing that, Megan. I'm so pleased with your progress. I know it's been brief, but it's been a pleasure to work with you these last few months.'

He stands and indicates that I can go. I move towards the door. This is it. The last time I'll see him. I want to show Mr Harwell how grateful I am. I pause, hand resting on the handle. Do it, Megan. Do it! I can feel him staring at me. If he speaks, asks me if there's anything else, I'll lose my nerve. But there's nothing. Just an expectant pause.

I turn, force myself to look up and meet Mr Harwell's gaze. I part my lips, slide my tongue between my teeth, and mouth the words 'Thank you' at him.

For a moment, Mr Harwell's expression is frozen. Then his eyes widen, two spots of colour darken his cheeks, and he smiles. 'You're doing so well, Megan. One day you're going to talk again.'

You won't. Because you know what will happen if you do.

I catch my breath, almost choke on it. Then, with a massive effort, I push the voice aside, look at Mr Harwell, and grin.

Finally, at the end of June, the exams are over, and a gloriously long summer stretches out before us. On one of the hottest days of the year, Jasmine announces that her family are having a barbecue at the weekend. 'Mum's gone completely over the top. She's invited the whole village. Literally. She put an advert up at the Post Office. I can't wait, though, Megan. It's going to be so much fun!'

I'm excited, too. Almost as excited as Mum, though she's having a crisis about what to wear. 'I want to look nice, Megan, but not tarty. Do you know what I mean? Don't want it to look like I've made a huge effort, but I want to give a good impression. Is gold too tacky? Should I go for heels or wedges? What do you think? Too much?' She puts this low-cut pink thing on the bed.

I nod. Definitely too much. Too much of everything, especially the cleavage. I pick out a navy dress with a print of swooping swallows and lay it over the pink monstrosity.

Mum screws up her face. 'I wore that to Aunt Mary's funeral.'

I try not to laugh. Mum catches my eye. She's trying not to laugh too. 'It's not funny!' she giggles. 'It's so not funny!'

On Saturday, Mum spends ages putting her face on. I write her a note to say she looks nice. She hasn't overdone it and gone all orange, which is a relief. She smiles and returns the compliment, souring it slightly by asking if I want to do something different with my hair.

Clutching a bottle of cheap red wine and a bowl of mixed salad (emptied straight from a bag), we set off to Jasmine's just after noon.

When we arrive, Eleni hurries over. 'Hi!' she says, pulling me into a hug. 'Welcome. *Kalos orísate.*' She smells of vanilla today, like the buttercream frosting Grandpa used to whip up for his cakes.

Eleni introduces herself to Mum, then drags her away to meet people. She calls over her shoulder that Jasmine's 'around somewhere'.

I'm on my own. I put my hands in my pockets and try to look relaxed. There are loads of people here. Most of them I recognise, including – oh, God – Sadie's parents. Does that mean she's here as well? I scan the garden. There she is, with Lindsay, both looking like they're standing barefoot in a vat of frogspawn.

Sadie says loudly to her mum, 'This is the lamest party ever. Can I go now?'

I try to walk past so I can hide inside, but Sadie's mum, Annemarie, spots me. 'Megan! I haven't seen you in ages!' She's a pretty blonde with small, intelligent eyes and a pear-shaped birthmark on her right cheek.

Most of the adults stop talking and look at me. There's a spotlight shining in my face. *Please stop looking at me.*

Annemarie starts to ask how I am, then trails off when she realises she won't get an answer. There's a painful silence. It stretches on for ever, until she clears her throat and says, 'It was lovely to see you. I hope you're doing OK.' She touches my shoulder lightly, then allows me to leave.

I instruct my legs to unlock and hurry inside to look for Jasmine. Seriously, where is she?

'All right, freak?' Sadie follows me, sauntering into Jasmine's kitchen like she owns the place.

Jasmine, where are you?

Sadie looks down her nose at the chaos on the work surfaces. 'What a dump.'

Shut up!

She pokes a *kofte* on a plate. 'Sick. They look like turds.'

Just shut up!

I try to yank the plate away from her, but it slips through my fingers and shatters on the floor.

'What the hell?' Sadie shouts, flicking pieces of minced lamb and crockery off her bare legs.

Lily comes in. 'What's going on?' she says, taking in the mess. When neither of us answer, she asks Sadie, 'Who are you?'

Sadie gives her a cold look. 'Nobody you need to worry about. I won't be coming here again.' She struts out of the kitchen.

Lily makes a face. 'What's the matter with her?'

I shrug.

Lily shows me where the dustpan is, then helps me clear up. I wish I could apologise, but sweet little Lily smiles in a way that suggests I don't need to.

Afterwards, she picks up a plate of halloumi, grins and says, 'Yummy! Dad's going to start cooking now!' I manage to raise a smile, then head upstairs to the bathroom.

I pause to look out of the window on the upstairs landing,

wondering if there are any more people arriving. And then I see Jasmine. She's on the pavement outside, talking to Owen. I can't believe her! She's abandoned me for him again. How could she?

I watch them for a few minutes, my angry breaths steaming up the glass. I hate the way she keeps laughing and touching his arm. Owen's been hanging around like a bad smell for the last few weeks, whenever we walk to the bus stop. The only time I get Jasmine to myself is on the bus. Well, I hope she's been having fun while I've been left alone to deal with Sadie.

I lock myself in the bathroom for a few minutes and try some of Mr Harwell's relaxation techniques. I should probably go home. I'm not in the mood now.

I pad down the stairs. Someone's singing in the kitchen. I stop. It's Jasmine. She has the most amazing voice. I listen for a moment, then peek round the door.

Jasmine has her back to me. A knife clacks against a chopping board. She's wearing a pair of denim cut-offs and a fuchsia top. Her hair is swept to one side, her shining curls flowing across her shoulder. I watch, just for a moment, resisting the urge to stroke the nape of her neck.

Jasmine whips round and shrieks. 'Megan! You scared me!' She clutches her chest theatrically, but she's smiling. 'Want a carrot stick?' Not waiting for an answer, she pops one in my mouth. When her fingers graze my lips, my heart skips. I thought I was cross, but I don't know what I feel now.

'Thank God you're here. Mum has been treating me like a slave for the whole morning. I swear if I have to peel another flipping carrot, I'm going to jab someone's eye out. Who's here? Has anyone from school turned up?'

I look around for something to write on. Jasmine gives me an old shopping list. She scowls when she sees what I've written.

'You're joking.'

I shake my head.

'Who asked them? Well, Mum, obviously, but why did they come?'

I write: *Maybe their parents made them?*

Jasmine pauses for a moment, winding one of her curls around a finger, then flits to another topic. She's like a butterfly that can't settle on one flower.

'Mum's made about a thousand dips. The woman's mad! We're going to be eating leftovers for a week. You'll take some home, won't you? Don't leave it all here with us. I'll be the size of a house by next weekend!'

I nod.

'I'm starving! Hope Dad cooks the *sheftalia* soon.'

I peer at a packet of meatballs with strings of fat wrapped round them, trying to look open minded.

Jasmine laughs. 'They're nice, honest. Better than those nasty tinned things you like!'

Nothing wrong with frankfurters.

Jasmine strokes my shoulder and throws me a cute little smile. I grin back, feeling a trail of heat where she touched me. I definitely don't want to go home now. I wish we could stay here for the rest of the barbecue.

'Hey, I've got that jacket in my room – the one that will

totally look better on you. It's miles too small for me, but it'll look great on you. Want to pop up and try it on?'

I nod and follow Jasmine up the stairs. She pushes the door to her room open and stops in her tracks. I walk into her. I hear her breath hitch. 'What ... what is this?' she says shakily.

I move around Jasmine so I can see. Oh my God. Someone's slashed all of her posters. It looks like they've used a knife and just cut them, right down the middle. Half of Audrey Hepburn's face has been sliced off. My stomach rolls with acid.

Jasmine reaches for my hand and clutches it tight. Her skin is clammy. 'I've had enough of this,' she says, squeezing even tighter. 'She has the nerve to show up at my house, eat my parents' food, then do this? She's gone way too far.'

Jasmine lets go of my hand, flies out of the room and pounds down the stairs.

No! I want to call after her, stop her, but all I can do is follow.

Jasmine storms into the garden and makes a beeline for Sadie, who doesn't even have a second to react before Jasmine's shaking her shoulders and shouting in her face: 'What are you playing at? Do you think that's funny? Do you seriously think that's funny?'

Conversations fall silent and all eyes turn to them. Sadie breathes heavily, her skin flushed. She looks at Jasmine as if she's lost her mind.

Lindsay is on the other side of the garden and strides towards them, her arms pumping, but – thank God – Eleni swoops in first, breaking the girls apart. 'What do you think you're doing, Jasmine?'

'She ruined my room!' Jasmine yells, her face red as she flings her arms around. I swallow heavily. I've never seen her like this before. 'I'm sick of her! Why did you even invite her?'

Eleni firmly grabs Jasmine's arms, forces her to lower them, then looks her straight in the eyes. When she speaks, her voice is low and measured. A couple of people move closer so they can hear what she says. 'I don't know what's happened, but we'll talk about it later. You need to cool down in your room.'

Jasmine looks past her mum to Sadie, who glares back as she adjusts her crumpled clothes. 'I haven't been upstairs at all,' she says. 'You've lost it.'

Annemarie lays a hand on her daughter's shoulder. 'I don't quite know what Sadie's being accused of, but she's only been inside once since we got here, and that was just for a minute. She came straight out again.'

Just a minute? That must've been when she followed me in. But if it wasn't Sadie, who was it? I glance at Lindsay, who's staring daggers at Jasmine.

'I'm so sorry,' Eleni says, smiling. 'There's obviously been a misunderstanding.'

Jasmine heads inside. I hesitate for a moment, then follow. She's crying before she even starts up the stairs. I wait until we're in her room, then I put my arms around her.

'It's not the posters I'm bothered about,' she says. 'I can replace those. It's the fact that she came into my room. My space.'

I nod. I understand.

'I can't tell Mum,' Jasmine murmurs, almost to herself. 'I know what she'll do. We'll be out of here.'

I put some music on – one of Jasmine's favourite albums – and we lie on the bed, side by side, listening to it, our hands clasped.

'Thank you,' Jasmine whispers. 'I don't know what I'd do without you.'

She's so close her hair is tickling my ear. There's a stray tear on her cheek. I reach up, about to stroke it away.

'Jasmine!' Eleni calls up the stairs. Jasmine jumps and sits up. 'You can come down now.' From the tone of Eleni's voice, Jasmine doesn't have much choice but to go.

'You coming?'

I shake my head, pull my notepad out and write: *I'll stay here. Sort this mess out.* I point at the mutilated posters.

Her eyes soften. 'Would you? You're amazing, Megan.'

I blush and try to hide my massive grin.

A few minutes later, as I'm peeling the last poster from the wall, there's a quiet knock on the door. I open it. It's Luke. I stare at him for a moment, surprised, but manage to find a smile.

Luke runs his fingers through his tousled hair. He's dressed casually, but I can tell he's made an effort today. His T-shirt shows off the nice shape at the tops of his arms, and he's wearing a pair of very white, new trainers.

'Hi, thought you might be up here. OK for me to come in?'

I shrug, feeling a bit awkward about inviting him into someone else's room.

Luke gestures towards the bed. 'Shall we … sit down or something?'

I nod.

Luke sits. He doesn't mention the pile of poster scraps on the floor.

'So, how are you? Haven't really spoken to you in ages.'

A bit freaked out, if I'm honest.

Luke stares at the floor. He looks like he's struggling with something, so I wait.

'There's this thing I've wanted to do for ages. And I … ' He breaks off and laughs, then shuffles towards me, until he's so close the soft hairs on his arms brush against mine. There's a tiny scar next to his nose. Why haven't I noticed it before? Luke gives me a nervous smile. 'For some reason, I woke up and decided that today was the day.'

Ever so gently, slowly, he grasps my chin, tilting it towards him. His eyes meet mine. I'm trapped. I can't look away.

What are you doing?

His voice is husky. 'I really, really want to kiss you.'

Eh?

Before I can even begin to process what's happening, he leans forward and presses his lips against mine.

First kiss! My first kiss. It's … Wow! It's nice. Luke tastes of lemon. His stubble prickles me. He's tender, slow. Oh! There's his tongue. I wasn't expecting that! What do I do?

But he shows me. And it's nice. Really nice.

Luke pulls away. He's laughing! What did I do wrong? I'm actually going to die of embarrassment.

'Sorry,' he says. 'You have no idea how long I've wanted to do that.'

I redden and look away, but I'm smiling too.

'Will you go out with me?' Luke blurts. 'To the cinema or something.'

I'm nodding. Why am I nodding? What just happened?

Luke moves in for another kiss, but Jasmine calls up the stairs and he stops. 'Megan! Your mum's looking for you.'

Something dark flashes across Luke's eyes. Then they soften and he settles for a peck on the lips. 'You'd better go back down. How's next weekend?'

I nod and smile, wondering what the hell I'm doing.

CHAPTER EIGHTEEN

My date with Luke comes around quickly. Far too quickly. Jasmine is ecstatic about the whole thing, which, in a strange way, makes me even more determined to try things out with Luke.

Jasmine didn't even realise that Luke was at the barbecue. I think he disappeared soon after our kiss, which is just as well because Jasmine would've been teasing him about it all afternoon.

The kiss was sweet and lovely. Luke is sweet and lovely. But is he really what I want? I don't want to use him, hurt him, but how can I be sure until I've given things a go?

Luke takes me to the cinema in Bournemouth on Saturday afternoon. On the bus, his knee keeps knocking against mine. I don't know if he's doing it deliberately or if it's just because we're going over loads of potholes. I try to remember if his knee used to knock against mine when we were on the school bus, but it didn't matter as much then. Luke's hands rest on his thighs, but they look odd, like he's arranged them there. I wonder if he wants to hold my hand.

The bumps in the road are making my stomach squirm. I've been nauseous all morning.

'You look nice,' Luke says with a shy smile. 'Really pretty.'

I mentally thank Jasmine for making me wear this turquoise top. Bright colours aren't usually my thing, but I couldn't resist after she told me I looked hot in it.

'How did you get on with that new psychologist you had at school?' Luke asks.

I nod and write: *Really good. He got me to hum. Never thought I'd be able to do that again. I mean, I didn't think I'd be able to do it in front of other people.*

Luke stares out of the window for a moment, then turns to me and says, 'I miss hearing your voice, you know.'

I smile, managing to meet his gaze for a couple of seconds – enough to notice that Luke's light-blue shirt perfectly matches his eyes. He looks good as well. I should've told him, but it seems a bit lame to say it now.

At the cinema, we have a gentle argument about what to watch. I'm happy with this alien blockbuster that's just come out, but Luke insists he doesn't mind going for the teen romance based on some bestselling book. In the end, he gets his way. It's hard to win an argument when you can't speak.

He also insists on buying me snacks. I honestly don't think I could eat anything, so I end up choosing a kids' portion, which comes with a free plastic toy: an action figure with a massive, rippled torso and ridiculously small legs. Luke takes the piss, but he has great fun playing with it while we're waiting for the film to start, walking it up and down my arms, waving it around and making it talk in a high-pitched, girly voice. I giggle and roll my eyes. When people start giving us looks, I take it off him and put it in my bag. He pouts a bit and I resist the urge to push his lips into a smile.

While the trailers are on, I glance at a couple sitting not far away. They're about our age. The girl is pretty, with skin so black it almost shines. I like her long, tightly braided hair and wonder what it would feel like to run my fingers through it. Her boyfriend is whispering something in her ear and she's smiling a secret, sexy smile.

The film starts, but I can't really concentrate on it. Luke's hand is inching towards mine. A couple of times, he lifts it off his lap, leaves it hovering for a few moments, then puts it back again. About half an hour in, he makes a sudden move and grasps my hand. Then he relaxes.

My skin gets all hot and sweaty. It's so bad Luke has to let go and subtly wipe his palm on his jeans. My face flares up.

What's wrong with you?

I jump. I'm an idiot. That's what's wrong with me. I'm sitting here on a date with someone I don't know how I feel about. I'm possibly leading him on, I'm probably going to hurt him, and I might end up losing him as a friend.

Luke is persistent. He grabs my hand again and gives it a

gentle squeeze to let me know it's OK. His skin feels different to Jasmine's: more rough, as I'd expect from a boy, but also more bony, not quite as comfortable. Holding his hand is weird. And it doesn't get any less weird.

After the film, most of which I don't remember, we go to this Italian place near the cinema. It's nowhere special – it's in a shopping centre and has fake tomato vines on the walls – but the spaghetti carbonara is good.

Jasmine has sent loads of texts. I have a quick look when I go to the loo, just in case she's had any more nasty threats, but they're all about the date:

Has he kissed you yet?
Did he pay?
What's he wearing?
Did you sit on the back row?

I send her a quick reply, promising to tell her everything later.

When I get back to the table, Luke starts to talk about the film. I write him a note on a napkin to say: *I bet Jasmine would've loved it.*

Luke pauses, gives me this strange look and says, 'Yeah, well, she's not here.'

I stare at the green chequered tablecloth until my vision starts to blur. I can see Luke's hand clutching the edge of the table so hard the blood is draining from his fingertips. What did I do? Why is he so mad?

Then he takes a deep breath and releases his grip, one finger at a time. 'Sorry,' he says with a soft laugh. 'Don't even know why I said that! Hey, let's get some dessert.'

I groan and hold my stomach, shaking my head.

'C'mon. I've seen you devour one of those ice cream sundaes at Harry's. I know you have space for dessert. I even know that your favourite ice cream is caramel, especially if it's caramel swirl with fudge pieces. See? Impressed?'

I look up, catch his eye for a second and offer a quick smile. How did he even remember that?

I give in and we order a dessert to share. While we wait, Luke picks out a couple of cheesy lines from the film and mimics them in a stupid voice. I laugh. Luke makes me laugh a lot. And he makes me feel good about myself. But as he's chatting, all I'm doing is trying to figure out how to explain that it doesn't feel right.

We catch the bus back to Brookby. Luke is struggling to keep the conversation going. I think he's just about exhausted every topic, from orienteering, to sailing, to football. 'This is really embarrassing,' he admits. 'All I've done is go on about me. I'm sick of hearing my own voice!'

I smile.

'I hear you've taken some wicked photos. What kind of things do you photograph?'

The forest, mostly, I write. *Animals, trees, the heath.*

'Can I see them some time?'

I nod, though I'm not sure he'll feel the same after I've let him down. Oh, Luke. Please don't be too hurt. I don't want to lose you.

I'm a wreck on the walk home. Is he going to kiss me? What do I do? Maybe he won't. He is. I know he is. It's not fair to let him, but what's the other option? Try to explain with a note scrawled on the back of a cinema ticket? I can't do that. I need time to work out what I'm going to say. This is such a mess!

When we reach my house, Luke stops. He looks hopeful. Even though I shouldn't, a part of me does want him to kiss me again. Because it was nice the first time. Because it's just nice that someone wants to kiss me.

I take a brave step towards him and close my eyes. I feel his breath on my face before I feel his lips. Then I relax. Luke's so good at this. I kind of sigh into his mouth: a happy sigh.

'Thanks for the date,' he whispers, his forehead resting on mine. 'Glad I finally got to take you out.'

Luke waits until I'm safely inside before he leaves.

I close the front door and lean back against it, my heart pumping way too fast.

Over the next few days, I think about the kisses a lot, and how much I liked them. But nice kisses aren't enough. It's not right. I know it's not right, so it's not fair to carry on. Luke's texted a couple of times. I've texted back, but avoided making any firm plans. I tried to write him a letter, but every version so far has ended up in the bin.

I wake one morning with flutters in my chest. Jasmine and I are going on a bike ride today. The air is still and it feels muggy, with grey clouds hanging low in the sky, but I can't wait to get out there and show off the forest. I want Jasmine to see it how I see it, to fall in love with it too.

Mum has never been into outdoorsy stuff, but when I was little, Grandpa and me used to walk together. I remember listening for the rustle of a sweet wrapper as he pulled a toffee from his pocket. He always had a treat in one pocket and a fistful of birdseed in the other.'You'll know I've lost my marbles when I get them mixed up!' he joked.

I loved the story of how Gran and Grandpa met. He used to tell me while we were walking, the lines beside his mouth creasing like crumpled paper as he smiled.'I met your Gran in 1940, during a blackout. We were sixteen. Both walking down the same road in the dark. We just got chatting. I knew then that she was the one.'

All I ever wanted was for someone to love me the way Grandpa loved Gran. He sent her photos of himself, when they were separated by the war, and wrote beautiful messages on the back: *Your heart will always be mine. All my love is yours.* Before he died, he asked to be buried with a lock of her hair, saying that he wanted a piece of her to always be with him.

I imagine telling Grandpa how I feel about Jasmine. 'You can't help who you fall for,' he'd probably say. Then he'd gaze at Gran with that adoring expression he reserved just for her.

'Megan!' Mum bellows.

I jump.

'Jasmine's here!'

She's here!

'Megan? Are you awake?'

I loiter in my bedroom doorway, unwilling to venture out in case Jasmine sees me looking like a state.

Mum comes up. She takes in my creased pyjamas and unbrushed hair. 'Oh, she's going to be a while, Jasmine. She's not even dressed. Why don't we have a cuppa?'

I rush to the bathroom and grab my toothbrush. Jasmine's voice floats up the stairs. Suddenly I can't wait to leave. I spit out the toothpaste, not even bothering to rinse properly.

Ten minutes later, I bound down the stairs and leap over the last one, slapping my bare feet on the floorboards.

Mum's face pops round the kitchen door. 'Someone's in a good mood. Why haven't you got any socks on?'

I pad through to the kitchen, manage a small wave and smile at Jasmine, grab a leaflet about a garden fête, and scribble *wash load* on the back.

Mum sighs. 'Sorry, love. I completely forgot. I'll do one today.'

I tap Jasmine's arm and point to the door. She unwraps her fingers from the mug of tea she's cradling, slips off the chair and follows me. I sneak a little glance. She's wearing a pistachio-coloured jumper. Her red coat completely clashes with it, but follows the gorgeous inward swoop of her waist.

'Wait a minute!' Mum calls. 'Aren't you going to eat anything before you go?'

I shake my head.

'Don't worry, my mum packed us loads of food.' Jasmine rattles her backpack. 'We're not going to starve.'

For a moment, Mum looks disgruntled, until a smile darts across her face. 'I've got something you can have!' She pulls a couple of cans of cheap cola out the fridge and rummages around the biscuit barrel until she finds two crummy Penguin bars that have been festering there for ever.

Jasmine is going to be a great actress. The way she grins and thanks Mum, you'd think she'd just been presented with a gourmet hamper.

Outside, a puff of air whispers through my hair. The clouds are breaking apart. Across the road, Mrs Newman is loading a bin bag with cut grass and the breeze is full of its sweet summer scent.

Jasmine needs a little coaxing to get on the bike that Mum's lent her. At first she just shrieks and wobbles a few metres down the street, before planting her feet back on the ground, crossing her arms and declaring, 'I can't do it! I just can't do it!'

I stand beside her, pat the handlebars and try to smile encouragingly.

'It's no use, Megan. I have no sense of balance. I'm rubbish at it!'

I shake my head and push the handlebar forward. Jasmine chews her lower lip, her forehead furrowed as she concentrates. Her feet find the pedals and she starts to cycle unsteadily on her own. 'I'm going to fall off. I just know it! Stay next to me, won't you?'

I start to run beside her, my body tensing when she teeters and looks like she might go over. But Jasmine rights herself, laughing under her breath. 'This isn't so bad.'

She executes a shaky turn and we head back to my house to pick up my bike.

'You won't go too fast?' Jasmine asks, her eyes wide. 'You won't race off without me?'

I shake my head.

Jasmine draws in a deep breath. When she releases it, I can smell her crisp mint mouthwash. 'OK. I think I'm ready to go now.' She lifts her feet, sways, then pumps the pedals, whooping as she picks up speed.

I smile and follow her. I catch up at the end of the road, where Jasmine is wrestling with the gate. 'I've never lived anywhere with so many flipping gates and grids!' she huffs.

I get off my bike to help her. A few months ago, someone forgot to close the gate and a couple of donkeys got in. I was woken by Mrs Newman screaming because they'd pooed on her lawn and nibbled chunks out of her hedge.

In the village centre, we ride past the tat shops, their windows festooned with creepy puppets whose painted eyes peer out at us.

'They seriously scare me, those things,' Jasmine shouts. 'They're like something from a horror film! I bet they come to life at night and sneak into people's houses.'

I smile and shake my head.

As soon as we leave the village and get out in the open, I feel like I'm filling with hundreds of tiny bubbles. I could almost laugh out loud. I stop to take a photo of the heath, which stretches towards the horizon in a collage of yellows, browns and greens. The sky is slowly clearing and a streak of light pokes through a gap in the clouds. There are hints of a blue sky hiding behind them.

I catch up with Jasmine. She seems to be more confident on the bike, until a car races past, too close, and she screams and almost falls off. My heart squeezes and stops for a moment, but she's OK. Jasmine regains her balance, then yells, 'Next time why don't you try to knock me into the bloody ditch?'

Ahead, a brazen pony stands in the middle of the road, coolly eyeing the tourists who slow down to gawp at it. I swerve around and overtake Jasmine so I can lead her to one of my favourite spots. I hear her shout, 'No zooming off! I don't want to be left behind.'

We turn into a side road, barely wide enough to fit a car. The tarmac is old and crumbly, and a mohawk of grass has sprouted down the middle. As it becomes a hill, Jasmine starts to moan. 'I'm hot . . . I'm tired . . . My legs ache.'

I reply in my head, over and over again: *Just wait until we get to the top.*

When we reach it, I hope Jasmine can see why it's worth the effort. The view sweeps into the distance, sliced in two by a silver river whose banks are peppered with the shadows of grazing cows. A couple of swans barely disturb the mirrored surface as they drift through the water, necks bent in elegant arcs.

'Oh, Megan,' Jasmine breathes. 'It's beautiful. It makes you feel tiny, doesn't it?'

I never feel tiny when I'm with you.

Unusually for Jasmine, she allows a silence to settle between us. We listen to the wind ruffle through leaves, birds chirping and twittering, the hum of the road.

Jasmine stirs and stretches as if she's just waking up. 'There's this place in Cyprus, up in the mountains, where you can see everything – literally everything – for miles: olive groves, lemon trees, villages with white houses and orange roofs. The whole works! If you ever visit, I'm taking you up there. We'll go and see *Yiayiá*. I'll get her to make ladies' fingers. We could maybe stop at a taverna for moussaka, walk one of the waterfall trails. You'd love it, Megan. I swear.'

I smile, not quite meeting Jasmine's eyes. *It sounds amazing. I'd love to go with you.*

Jasmine's skin is glowing from the exercise. Her lips seem darker, more full. An errant curl has escaped from her ponytail and is resting on her cheek.

I want to tuck it behind her ear.

I want to do more than that. I want to kiss her. I want her to kiss me back. I don't care what the consequences are. I just want to kiss her.

You're going to mess it all up.

I can't kiss her. There's no way I can kiss her.

I take a step back, lock my hands at my sides. If I get carried away, I'll scare Jasmine off, lose her as a friend. I'll spoil everything.

CHAPTER NINETEEN

Dear Luke,

I'm sorry for sticking this through your door. Sorry I didn't have the guts to deliver it face to face. I guess you know what's coming. I know this is a horrible way of telling you. Believe me, if I had the words, I'd use them. This is totally about me. I know it's a cliché. 'It's not you, it's me!' But it really is.

You're a lovely, funny, sweet guy and I had the best time with you, but it's just not right. I'm sorry.

Is there any chance we can still be friends? I'm hoping that, maybe, after the summer, you'll have forgotten all about me and found someone who really deserves you.

Thanks for the cinema trip and the meal. And the action figure, too. I like it more than I let on.

See you around,

Megan

CHAPTER TWENTY

I'm such a coward. I actually run from Luke's house after I've posted the letter. What if his mum reads it? What if Luke stays with his dad this week and doesn't see it until the weekend? What if I bump into him before then and he tries to kiss me again?

I head straight for Jasmine's to confess what I've done.

She starts tidying her bedroom, swiping up dirty clothes and hurling them at her wash basket. 'I just don't get it, Megan. The guy's crazy about you. Plus, he's like the perfect man.'

She doesn't say it, but I know she's wondering what's wrong with me.

I write on the back of a magazine: *But I don't feel the same about him. It's cruel to lead him on. I don't get why you like Owen so much, but I don't go on about it.*

'Well, that's different!'

No, it isn't, I reply. *I don't try to tell you how to feel.*

Jasmine flops down next to me on the bed. 'I'm not trying to tell you how to feel … am I? Oh, I don't know. I'm sorry. I'm doing that bossy thing again. I just want you to be happy.'

I scribble in quick, angry strokes: *Does Owen make you happy?*

'What's your problem with Owen?'

Nothing, I write. *I just don't want you to get hurt.*

'Look, I know I can't exactly bring him home to meet my parents, but there's just something about him, you know?'

No, I really don't. But I'm not writing that down.

We sit in silence for a few moments, then Jasmine pokes me in the ribs. When I look up, she sticks her tongue out. I grin, pick up a pillow and whack her in the face. She squeals and lunges at me, tickling me around the waist. I try to get away, but Jasmine leaps on top of me, pinning me to the bed. I twist beneath her, but I can't stop laughing. She's laughing too, breathless and beautiful.

Jasmine stops and looks at me for a long moment. The atmosphere changes, grows serious again. Neither of us looks away. Then Jasmine hoists herself off and puts the radio on, loud.

'Let's dance!' she says. 'C'mon. I want to dance!'

I laugh. There's no music – the DJ is just talking – but Jasmine starts to bounce around the room to an imaginary beat. I get up and grab her hands, leaping up and down with her, shaking my head from side to side. We don't care how stupid we look. When we're out of breath, we collapse on the bed, giggling helplessly.

Jasmine goes to fetch some drinks and I grab my pen, eager to share an idea I've had. When she gets back, I thrust a note at her: *Fancy going camping for my birthday? Grandpa used to be mates with this farmer who said we could pitch our tent in his field for free. We could use Grandpa's old tent. It's a bit musty but I reckon it'll be fine. There's loads of camping gear, too.*

'I think it's a great idea!' Jasmine declares. 'I used to go hiking and camping all the time in Cyprus. It's going to be so much fun! I can get one of those blow-up mattresses so we don't have to sleep on the ground. We should have proper camping food, like sausages and beans. Oh! And marshmallows. There *has* to be marshmallows. I burnt my lip on one once. It blistered and looked ugly for days. Still love them, though. When they get a bit black and crispy on the outside, but they're all gooey and warm on the inside – lush!'

We spend the rest of the afternoon making plans and lists of what we'll take.

As I'm walking home, I wonder whether Luke has got my letter yet. It's awful not knowing. How does he feel about me now? Does he hate me, or does he still really like me? If I were a normal person, I'd just make up a reason to call him. If I could just talk to him, I'd know how he was feeling.

I should've asked Jasmine to call him. But things seem a little off between them. I wonder why he didn't even say hi to her at the barbecue. Hang on a minute ... what if he did? What if he made a move on her, and she rejected him, and that's why he came and found me? No. Jasmine would've told me. She wouldn't have kept that a secret. God! Talk about paranoid!

After dinner, I get a text from Luke. My finger hovers over the 'open' button. I have no idea how he's going to react. Anger? Hurt? Spite? No, not spite. That's not Luke's style. I open it:

Got your note. OK.

That's it? Clearly, it's not OK. What am I supposed to do now? Go round? No. Too soon. Maybe in a couple of weeks.

I get a second text. I open it quickly, heart thudding:

BTW, changing my number soon. Will text you the new one.

Why do I get the distinct impression he'll never send me that number? I've lost him. Screwed things up, as usual. But he'll still keep our secret safe, won't he? He promised. We both did.

You'd better not break that promise.

The next morning, I ask Mum about the camping trip. She stares down at her fingers, picking at some chipped nail polish. 'Well, I had booked your birthday off, Megan. I thought we'd do something together.'

Oh no. Really? Now I feel bad.

'It's fine. I'll give Carolyn a call. See if she wants to go for coffee.'

I write on the back of a bill: *You sure?*

'Yes. It's all right. You and Jasmine don't want me cramping your style.' Mum smiles unconvincingly. 'You're becoming inseparable. You can have dinner under the stars. How romantic!'

What does that mean? Does she know? How does she know? Am I that obvious? Does Jasmine know too?

The doorbell rings several times, then Jasmine lets herself in. She rushes into the kitchen, hair astray and cheeks glowing. She's breathing heavily, as if she's run all the way here. 'Look what I found!' she gasps, slamming something on the table.

Mum and I peer at a crinkled page torn from the local paper. It's an article about a Polish artist who makes sculptures from old coat hangers.

'Not that!' Jasmine pokes a red finger at the bottom of the page. 'That!'

It's an advert for a competition: Hampshire Young Wildlife Photographer of the Year. My pulse quickens. I scan the rules. I'm eligible. I check out the prize: to have my photo on display in a local gallery. But I'm shaking my head. There's no way. I'm not good enough. Hundreds of people will enter. I won't stand a chance.

Mum and Jasmine are nodding and smiling.

'You *have* to enter, Megan. You're an amazing photographer!'

'Grandpa would be so proud,' Mum adds. 'You could use his old camera. He would've liked that.'

She's right. And he would've told me to go for it.

'Doesn't it have to be digital?' Jasmine asks.

Mum skims the small print. 'Doesn't say, so I guess not.'

I point to the clock. Mum's running eight minutes late. Her boss will be fuming.

'Oh, sod him!' she says. 'Man's so uptight you could press trousers in his arse crack!'

There's a moment of shocked silence. Then we all burst into laughter.

After Mum has left, Jasmine's mobile rings. She moves into the living room to answer it, but I can hear everything she's saying. 'I'm with Megan ... What do you mean, "again"? She's my best friend ... Don't be like that. I'll see you tomorrow ... No, you don't need to come round ... Yeah, I know it's strange that I'm just next door ... OK. Yep. Bye.'

She returns to the kitchen, sighing. 'I think he's going to dump me.'

Dump her? My heart does a little dance. Then I instantly feel guilty. What sort of friend wants her mate to be dumped?

Why? I write.

'I dunno. He's just been all grumpy recently. I think he might've gone off me because I've put on weight.'

What? I think. *What are you on about?*

'Look at his ex! Sadie's a stick insect compared with me!'

I scribble: *Sadie's a stick insect compared with anyone!*

Jasmine laughs, but it doesn't reach her eyes.

I start to write something, but end up scratching it out. This is so frustrating. I need words! How do I tell her?

You don't. Ever.

Jasmine squeezes my shoulder. 'Don't feel bad. I know I should lose a few pounds.'

But you shouldn't, I think. *You're beautiful. How do I show you?*

I have an idea, and jot it down: *Will you let me take some pictures of you?*

Portraits aren't my thing, but if I'm going to photograph anyone, I want it to be Jasmine.

She shakes her head, curling her arms around her waist. I want to hold her so badly. 'I really don't like it, Megan. I don't even like looking in the mirror.'

Please? I write. *Trust me?*

Jasmine considers for moment, then relents. 'OK. But only my top half. My boobs are the one thing I am proud of!'

We ride out to a small copse to take the photos. When we get there, Jasmine is restless. She tugs at her top, then asks if she can go home and change. I shake my head. Jasmine's wearing a necklace that Owen bought her. She adores it, but I think it looks a bit cheap. I make something up about it catching the light and ask her to take it off, putting it in my pocket.

I position Jasmine against a tree trunk, then gather up her mass of curls and draw them across one shoulder, where they spill down in glorious waves. I lay two fingers on the bottom of her chin, feel a small thrill at the touch of her skin beneath mine, and tilt it upwards, so she's looking towards the light.

Jasmine's eyes flicker down to meet mine and she smiles a smile that makes my heart falter. I point up and her gaze follows. I position the camera, frame the shot, and take a second to look at her. The sunlight darts across Jasmine's face and her eyes shine with the reflection of leaves above. She is stunning.

Jasmine notices I've paused. 'Is it OK? Am I doing it right?'

Perfect. You're perfect.

I keep taking shots until Jasmine yawns and says, 'Are we done yet? Can we get an ice cream now?'

I hold up a finger and pull my mobile out to take an instant shot of her. Jasmine leans in close, her breath whispering past my cheek. She gasps. 'Megan! You ... I don't know what to say! You've made me look ... I'm ... I look great!'

You're beautiful. I didn't 'make' you look anything.

We detour through the village to get ice creams, then amble back to Jasmine's.

'So I won't see you tomorrow,' she says. 'The day after, though?'

I nod and wave, keeping the smile on my face until I've turned round. So Owen wins tomorrow. What am I supposed to do? I hate having to share Jasmine. I hate that she makes me feel like this, but I can't say or do anything about it.

My head's all muddled, and it's a good evening for walking, so I wander around, keeping a constant eye out for Luke. The way I feel right now, I'd rather see Sadie than him, and that's saying something.

It's dark when I remember that I've still got Jasmine's necklace in my pocket. Owen will probably be annoyed if she's not wearing it tomorrow. Maybe I should keep it? No. That's horrible. What's wrong with me? Anyway, if I take it back it's a good excuse to see her again.

I'm almost at Jasmine's when the quiet road is pierced by a scream. Jasmine! My stomach lurches and I sprint to her house. When I get there, she's standing inside, the front door open, looking at something on the step. What is it? I can't see. It's too dark. Is she hurt? What should I do?

Jasmine's illuminated by a pool of light inside the house. She looks up at me, unsure for a moment. 'Megan? What are you ... Why are you here?' I take a step towards her. Jasmine steps back, closes the door a little. What's the matter with her?

'Why are you here, Megan?' she shouts, tears rolling down her face.

I reach into my pocket and pull out the necklace.

Jasmine squints through the night, then nods slowly. 'Have you seen this?' She gestures at the doorstep with a shaking hand.

I move towards her, then cover my mouth, swallowing the urge to vomit. It's a dead cat. I think its neck is broken. It's mangy. Probably a stray.

Jasmine is wailing, her hands clamped around the door to stop herself from falling. 'Who could do this? Why? What have they got against me?'

I shake my head. *I don't know. Oh, God, Jasmine. I don't know.*

Jasmine holds out a note. I have to lean over the cat to take it:

I DON'T WANT TO HURT YOU. I DIDN'T WANT TO HURT THE CAT EITHER, BUT LOOK WHAT HAPPENED.

CHAPTER TWENTY-ONE

Where are your parents? I write.

Jasmine just stares at my message. I touch her arm. She looks at me, but doesn't see me. She shudders, then seems to come back. 'They're ... um ... Where are they? They've taken Lily to the cinema.'

How did you find the cat?

'I ... er ...' Jasmine closes her eyes. Opens them again. 'Someone rang the doorbell, but there was no one here.'

They must've known her family were out. How did they know? Were they watching her? Are they still watching now? I glance up and down the road, but there's no one around. The hairs on the back of my neck prickle.

I'll stay with you until they're back, I write. *Can you get me a bin bag? I'll sort it out.* I smile, try to look calm, but I feel sick and shaky. Why does someone have it in for my best friend? And if they can kill a cat, what else are they capable of?

After I've cleaned up, I go through the house, switching on lights, the TV and the radio. Jasmine tries to call Eleni, but her mobile's off. I make her tea, stroke her hair, but I can tell she just wants her mum.

We try to watch something on TV, but Jasmine's not following it. She doesn't even flinch when a celebrity lies in a bath of maggots for charity.

The second the door opens, Jasmine launches herself at Eleni, weeping.

'What on earth . . . ?' Eleni asks, instantly enfolding Jasmine in her arms.

Between sobs, Jasmine explains what happened. Eleni reels off a furious string of Greek. Arthur sinks on to the sofa, cradling his head in his hands. Lily is sent to bed, though she doesn't give in without a fight. 'You can't make me go. I want to stay here with Jasmine.' She plonks herself on Jasmine's lap and throws her little arms around Jasmine's neck. Eleni gently pulls her away and takes her upstairs, leaving Jasmine, Arthur and me in shocked silence.

'We're calling the police,' Eleni announces when she returns. 'You should've told us sooner, Jasmine. This person has been in our house, in your room!'

'I thought it was just someone from school mucking around,' Jasmine says. 'I didn't realise they'd go this far.'

'Well, it's not going any further. I'm calling them right now.'

'Mum?' Jasmine asks. 'You're not going to make us move

again, are you?' She glances at me, and my heart breaks a little. 'I don't want to leave!'

Eleni and Arthur exchange a look. 'That's not up for discussion tonight,' Arthur says. 'One thing at a time.'

I can't look at Jasmine any more. She's devastated. I'm devastated. I can't even think about what would happen if she left.

Over an hour later, a police officer arrives. He takes a statement, but seems pretty disinterested. 'These types of incidents are usually kids playing pranks,' he says. 'I'll look into it, but I'm fairly confident they'll soon get bored.'

He gives Jasmine what he thinks is a reassuring smile. Patronising git!

Eleni stands abruptly. 'Well, thank you for your time, Officer,' she says in a clipped tone. 'I think we could all do with some rest now.' She ushers him to the door, then slams it behind him.

Jasmine and I leave her ranting to Arthur, alternating between Greek and English so fast it's hard to catch any of what she's saying.

I should go, I write. *Text me if you need anything.*

Jasmine nods and leans in for a hug. I clutch her tightly, holding on for longer than I should, but tonight, she doesn't seem to notice.

I lie awake. Tomorrow will not be a good day. The eleventh of July: Hana's birthday. Except she won't be turning sixteen. I can't get my head around that. When we were kids, Hana thought it gave her the right to win any argument. If she knew she was losing, she'd come back with: 'You have to listen to me –

I'm the oldest!' Not any more. She'll stay fifteen for ever, and in a few days, I'll be a year older than her, instead of a few days younger.

When I wake the next morning, there's a few seconds of blissful ignorance before it clicks. Then a wave of grief rolls over me and I turn on to my front so I can cry into my pillow. I think about Hana's last letter. Was she angry? Probably. I can guess what it said. I wish I'd found it sooner. If Sadie had just showed up five minutes later ... What's the point, though? It's gone. I'll never know what she was thinking.

Mum clatters around in the kitchen. 'Megan!' she yells. 'I'm off soon. You coming down?'

Of course, she's completely forgotten what day it is. Not so easy for Hana's parents, wherever they are. I imagine them in their new house, silently staring at each other across the breakfast table. Hana's mum is probably twisting her wedding ring around her finger. She always does that when she's stressed. I wish they'd kept in touch, after they moved. I miss them.

I wipe the tears from my face and get up. I try not to be mad with Mum. Why would she remember? It's not like it's my birthday.

I think about the parties that Hana and I had when we were kids: racing through tunnels or diving into ball pits at the play centre, splashing in the pirate ship or whizzing down flumes at the swimming pool, stuffing ourselves with doughnuts and screaming on rides at the theme park. By the time I get to the kitchen, I manage to muster a smile for Mum.

She is simultaneously wolfing down toast and applying

eyeshadow. 'I'm guessing you're heading over to Jasmine's today?'

I nod, grab some junk mail and write: *We're going to make camping plans!*

It's sweltering outside and the sky is cloudless. It's too hot to cycle to Jasmine's so I walk. Slowly. Within minutes, my clothes are clinging to me.

I knock on Jasmine's door and wait for someone to answer, feeling the usual flicker of excitement at seeing her again. But when Jasmine opens it, her face is downcast, her shoulders drooping. 'Hi,' she says in a sad, low voice.

I stare blankly.

Jasmine points inside and starts to head down the corridor. I grab her arm to make her look at me, frowning as questions dart through my mind. She just shrugs.

I feel it as soon as I step into the house. An atmosphere. I stop. My instinct is to leave. I don't want to barge into the middle of something.

Eleni appears from the kitchen. Everything about her face is pulled tight – her brow, lips, eyes. Her cheeks are coloured with two crimson circles. 'Hi, Megan. How are you?' she asks.

'She'll be pretty annoyed when I tell her how ridiculous you're being!' Jasmine snaps.

I step back, towards the door. Eleni sees me and shoots Jasmine a stern look. 'Will you just calm down? You're making Megan feel awkward.'

'I'm sorry, Megan, but she's being so unreasonable.'

Eleni throws her hands into the air. 'I won't apologise, Jasmine. I'm just not comfortable with it.'

I'm backed against the wall. I'm still not sure what's going on.

Jasmine swings round. 'She wants us to cancel the camping trip! She wants to ruin your whole birthday!'

'*Theé mou*! Stop being so dramatic! I'm just asking you to choose something else to celebrate your birthday, Megan. Given everything that's happened recently, with these strange notes and threats, I'd rather Jasmine stayed here.'

'That makes no sense! Whoever sent those notes knows that I live here! But nobody knows that Megan and I are going camping. How could they possibly find me?'

Eleni puts one hand on her hip and starts to wave the other at Jasmine. 'There's someone leaving dead cats on our doorstep and you expect me to let you camp in a field on your own? *Óchi*. No way.'

Jasmine's dad walks down the stairs with slow, measured steps. At the bottom, he stoops his lean body to avoid hitting the ceiling, then smiles at me, as if to say: *this is normal for them*.

'What do you think, Arthur?' Eleni demands.

'I've told you what I think,' he replies in his quiet, patient way.

'Then I don't want to hear it again.'

Jasmine senses an advantage and presses it. 'Dad, please. We won't be far from the main road. If anything happens, you could be with us in twenty minutes. I'll have my mobile and I'll check in with Mum as often as she wants.'

Arthur considers for a moment.

'Pleeeeaaaase?' Jasmine begs.

Arthur looks at Eleni and gestures towards the kitchen. She follows, but she's shaking her head and folding her arms as if nothing will change her mind.

I hold my breath as I catch snippets of what Jasmine's dad is saying. 'Under a lot of stress ... deserves a break ... policeman didn't seem to think ...'

When Eleni returns, her lips are pursed. 'Fine,' she agrees. Jasmine squeals. 'But one night, not two. And I want you to be in regular phone contact.'

As Eleni sweeps out of the room, Arthur receives a stony look. 'You know I won't sleep a wink while they're away,' she says in a stilted voice.

'Come on, Megan,' Jasmine shrieks, grabbing my hand and dragging me upstairs. 'We've got planning to do!'

When I get home, Mum has left a note to say she's gone to Southampton for a night out. I've been left to fend for myself as far as dinner goes. There isn't much in the house, but I don't have enough cash to buy anything, so I use a knife to chip out a pizza box that's stuck to the back of the freezer.

As the house fills with the smell of melting cheese, I set myself up for a night on the sofa. I'm glad Mum's gone out. I know she sometimes feels lonely, even when I'm with her. It must be nice to talk to someone she can actually have a conversation with.

I stay up to make sure she gets home OK. It's kind of funny

that the teenager is waiting up for the mum, but as the clock inches towards one, I start to lose my sense of humour.

I've just turned the TV off, ready to give up and go to bed, when the door crashes open, slamming into the wall behind it. I hear a giggle, followed by, 'Shhhh!'

I freeze. Who's she talking to? Please let her be talking to herself. She hasn't brought someone back, has she?

Oh God. She has. She really has.

There's another giggle, then a revolting wet sound as they snog in the hallway. Gross. Can't they see the living room light is on?

I get up, hoping to sneak past while they're distracted. But they stumble towards me, blocking my way. Mum and this man are pressed up against each other. They stink of booze.

This is wrong. So very wrong. I can't take any more of this. What do I do?

They're murmuring and laughing. I'm so glad I can't hear what they're saying. He's tugging her coat off and manages to get one arm out before he sees me.

'Bloody hell!' he shouts. 'There's a kid watching us!'

Mum looks up, lipstick smudged, boobs practically poking out of her sequinned top. She sways a little as she struggles to focus on me. 'Megan?' she mumbles. 'What you doing up?'

I sit back down on the sofa. A blush ravages my face. I don't look at her. Can't look at her.

'She were just standing there, watching us!' the bloke splutters. 'Who is she?'

'S'all right, she's my daughter.'

I glance up to see how he takes this. Not well. I don't think he realised Mum was old enough to have a teenage daughter.

'Look, let's just go up.' Mum grasps his collar and tries to draw him away.

God, Mum! How desperate are you?

But the man shakes her off and leans in towards me. His breath is rank. Beer and raw onions. I imagine him devouring a sweaty kebab and my stomach turns. 'What's the matter with you? Got no tongue?'

Mum grabs his shoulder, tries to pull him away. 'Come on. She doesn't talk.'

Her words pierce through me. I gasp and wrap my hands around myself. Why is she telling a complete stranger about me? It's none of his business. I see a glimmer of sobriety in her eyes – a moment of regret.

'What d'you mean, she don't talk?'

'Never mind. Forget it. Can't we just go upstairs?'

'Nah, I'm not in the mood any more. She's put me right off. What is she, an idiot or somefing?'

I pull my knees to my chest and bury my head in them.

You're nothing. Worthless.

I try to stifle a sob, but it escapes – a pathetic squeak. I'm nothing. Worthless.

Mum's response is so low and full of menace it's almost a growl. There's no trace of a drunken slur any more. 'Get the hell out of my house.'

'Yeah, no problem, love. Be happy to. Here's an idea: next time you pull, go back to his place.'

'Get the hell out of my house NOW!' Mum roars, unleashing a stream of swear words that fall down on him like fists, almost battering the man out of our house. He sneers at both of us, then swaggers outside. Mum stands on the doorstep and screams at him. The man's voice echoes down the street as he shoots back a string of foul words.

Mum slams the door.

I look up. Listen. He's gone. My hands unclench. I take a breath. I'm shaking. How could she do that to me? How could she bring that man into our house? She's supposed to protect me. I fly out of the living room, heading straight for the stairs.

'Megan, no!' Mum wails, reaching for me.

Leave me alone!

I shake her off, but she lunges at me again, grabbing my sleeve.

Get off! Don't touch me!

I elbow her. Hard. She cries out, trips over the telephone table, and thunks back into the door. There's a second of silence. I stop. Turn round. Mum's slumped on the floor, tears dragging inky mascara trails down her cheeks. I crouch down and clasp my hands around her neck, drawing her close, wrinkling my nose at the smell of stale fag smoke.

'Megan, my baby,' she cries. 'I'm sorry. So sorry for bringing that arsehole here. I keep messing up, Megan. I'm always messing up.'

I shake my head. *No, Mum. It's OK. I'm sorry I hurt you.*

I wish I could tell her. Now I'm sobbing too. My tears drip into her hair as we clutch each other.

When we're both done, Mum gently pushes me away so she can look at me. 'I bet *that* gave the neighbours something to talk about!' She grins. 'Did you hear him? What a potty mouth!'

I smile, help her to her feet, and we stagger up the stairs to bed.

I'm dreaming. I know I'm dreaming, but it's more than that. I'm remembering. Reliving. Someone is screaming. Is it me? Is she alive? Is there any way she's still alive? I can't see. Too many tears. Can't move. Too much pain. I didn't know I'd fallen, but someone hoists me up, their fingers pinching my arms. They're shaking me, shouting. I can't hear them. I can't hear anything but the voice.

It's your fault. You did this.

It's my fault. My fault that Hana's dead.

CHAPTER TWENTY-TWO

Dear Hana,

I'm sorry. I'm sorry.

I'm so, so sorry.

CHAPTER TWENTY-THREE

Dear Grandpa,

I just had the most horrible dream and I wish – I really wish – you were here. Remember that time I thought there was a snake in my room? I made you check everywhere: under the bed, in the cupboards, through all of my bedding. After you promised me there was nothing there, you took me downstairs, made me a mug of Horlicks, and sat me on your lap. You stroked my hair and whispered stories about how you wooed Gran by leaving little gifts for her to find on her walk to work.

I miss you so much. I can't deal with Hana being gone. I can't cope with what I did. I wish I could take it all back.

As if that wasn't enough, I'm falling for someone, and it's complicated. She's my best friend. I guess you'd be surprised that I like a girl, but I think you'd get used to it. You'd just want me to be happy. Maybe one day, I'll be as happy as you and Gran were.

Jasmine and I are going camping for my birthday. Being with her is brilliant, but it's scary too, in case I do something stupid. It's all so confusing. I'm such a mess, Grandpa.

If you see Hana, please tell her I'm sorry.

Megan xxx

CHAPTER TWENTY-FOUR

On the day before my birthday, Jasmine stops by on her way to Owen's. She's red-faced and her curls are sticking to her forehead, but she still looks great. 'Oh my God, Megan, the heat!' she says, fanning herself. It hasn't rained since the day Jasmine found the cat. 'I know I should be used to it, but on days like this in Cyprus, we'd just stay inside with the air-con on.'

We flop on to the sofa. I offer Jasmine a drink, but she shakes her head. 'I can't stay long. Owen's waiting.'

She brightens and suddenly claps her hands together. 'I just wanted to give you this!' With a flourish, Jasmine pulls a package from her bag, wrapped in polka-dot paper.

I scribble: *You know it's not until tomorrow, right?*

Jasmine grins. 'I know! But I can't wait any longer. Open it now! Open it now!'

I peel a piece of sticky tape off, careful not to let it tear the wrapping paper. I start to work on the next bit, hooking my nail beneath it. Jasmine has other ideas, though.'Just get on with it,' she says, ripping a huge chunk away.

I gasp, look at the gaping hole, and slap her lightly on the arm. Jasmine sticks her tongue out and moves closer, threatening to tear more. I rush to get there first, shredding the paper in a frenzy, throwing scraps in the air, laughing as they fall around us like confetti.

Jasmine's present is a beautiful photo album. I stroke the silky cover, tracing the oriental dragons snaking across it.

'Look inside!' Jasmine cries.

My mouth drops. Jasmine's taken my photos and arranged them for me, grouping them by theme, ordering them so the colours complement each other. I flick through, amazed. They look so good.

'Do you like it?'

I gaze up at her wonderful eyes, so wide and hopeful. I have to look away for a moment, worried I might cry. Then I draw Jasmine into a tight hug. I feel the thud of her heart against my chest. It would be so easy to just pull back a little, stroke her cheek and kiss her.

Jasmine unwraps her arms and points at the album.'I had to nick the photos from your room.Your mum helped me.'

You're so sweet.

I wish I could say it.

But you never will.

I really want to say it. *So sweet.*

When Mum gets in from work, I can't wait to show her what Jasmine's done.

'It's nice,' she says tersely, her eyes skimming across my photos. 'Really thoughtful. Not sure how I'm going to top it. I haven't got a clue.'

It's not a competition! Why can't you just be happy that Jasmine's done something special for me?

I head off to my room.

'What about a posh haircut?' Mum yells after me. 'You could have it dyed and restyled.'

I ignore her.

'Or you could get your nails done? You'd have to stop biting the bloody things for five minutes, though. They look horrible, Megan, all ragged and torn.'

I turn my music on, crank the volume up.

'You'll have to let me know what you want some time, you know,' Mum bellows. 'I'm not psychic.'

I cut the music. There's something more than frustration in her voice. Hurt? Guilt?

I hurry to the top of the stairs. Mum leans against the banister and smiles up at me. I write her a note, shape it into a paper aeroplane, and launch it towards her. Mum giggles as she catches it. She reads it, then nods. 'OK. You sure you want a rucksack, not a new handbag?'

I fix her with a look.

'OK, OK. A rucksack's fine. You can have what you want.'

*

When I wake the next day, the house smells of pancakes. Grandpa always used to make me pancakes on my birthday. In the kitchen, Mum is focusing on a sizzling pan. Flecks of batter are sprayed up the sides of the cooker, and there are two discarded pancakes in the bin: one that's thick enough to be a door wedge and another that's completely burnt.

Mum spins round. 'You made me jump!' she screeches. 'Happy birthday. We can pop into town and get the rucksack together – I'll only get the wrong thing. But here's a little something else.'

Mum picks up a package from the table. It's wrapped in a plastic bag with the words 'Madge's Mystical Emporium' on it. 'Sorry. I tried to get to the Post Office to buy proper wrapping paper, but that evil woman closed five minutes early. I told you, Megan, she's got it in for me. I banged on the door but she wouldn't open up. Old hag!'

I smile. I'm not bothered.

'So there's no card either. Sorry, sweetie. I'll make it up to you. Look! Pancakes!' Mum slides one on to my plate, then plonks a jar of syrup on the table. 'Hope they're OK.'

I take a large bite, smearing grease on my lips. It's a bit stodgy, but I give Mum the thumbs-up. At least she tried.

As I'm chewing, I peel away the plastic bag to reveal a book: a hardback with glossy photos of the New Forest. I put down my fork so I can pore over it. The shots are amazing: the framing, perspective, lighting. Everything is perfect.

'Thought it might give you some inspiration for that competition,' Mum says.

I smile. The closing date was a week ago. I haven't told her or Jasmine that I've entered. It'll be less embarrassing when I don't win.

I move over to give her a hug. Mum's hair smells of cooking oil. I grab a pen and an empty egg box and write: *Thanks. It's great.*

Eleni and Jasmine arrive later in a flurry of balloons and party poppers. Eleni brings a lovely, handmade card with a couple of appliquéd sheep on the front. Mum looks peeved, but doesn't say anything.

Jasmine has packed enough for a three-week trek in the Himalayas. Eleni sees me staring at all the stuff in her car boot and shakes her head. 'I know. I told her she didn't need four pairs of trousers, but she wouldn't listen.'

'You're the one who insisted I packed thermal underwear and water purifiers!' Jasmine says.

I try to shove my own gear around Jasmine's, but we end up emptying everything out so we can repack. Jasmine and Eleni bicker about the best way to fit the tent and camping stove in. I turn away, embarrassed.

Mum clacks down the path in a pair of silver stilettos. 'Are you ready?'

Eleni forces a smile. 'Yes, I think so.'

'Bye, baby,' Mum says. 'Enjoy yourself. Don't do anything I wouldn't!' She winks and giggles.

I roll my eyes. As if.

Mum kisses me on the forehead, then licks her finger to wipe off the lipstick she's left. I dart away and clamber into the back seat. The buckle on the seatbelt is so hot I almost cry out when

I touch it. I wind down both windows and we set off, Jasmine and Eleni's argument forgotten as they jabber about how Arthur is too chicken to go to the dentist, even though he's got really bad toothache.

'No toilets or showers,' Eleni teases when we get there. 'Are you sure you're going to manage?'

Jasmine sticks her nose in the air and ignores her.

Eleni stays to help us set up. Not that she's any good at it. Jasmine's the only one who knows what she's doing, and she loves bossing us both around.

When we're done, Eleni hesitates. 'I'll just check that rope is tight enough. Are you sure the beds are blown up properly? They look like they need more air. Shall we have a cup of tea before I head off? You can check the stove works.'

Even when Jasmine manages to persuade her that everything's fine, Eleni can't seem to stop fussing. 'Have you got enough toilet roll? I can always fetch you some more. It's the last thing you want to run out of. Oh, and Jasmine, did you check your mobile was fully charged? And did you bring that spare battery I bought for you?'

'Yes, Mum, the phone was charged for a full twelve hours last night, and I could hardly forget the spare battery, when you insisted on putting it in my bag.'

'OK.' Eleni's eyes flit to the ground. 'Well, I suppose I'd better get off.' She sweeps Jasmine into a hug.

'We'll be fine, Mum,' Jasmine mumbles. 'It's just one night.'

Eleni gives us both a weak smile, then heads back to her car.

Jasmine watches her leave. 'I don't know how to tell her I

want to backpack around Asia in my gap year,' she says. 'Anyway, what shall we do first, birthday girl? Do you fancy going for a walk, or do you just want to chill out here?'

I use my fingers to mime walking and she laughs. 'Don't know why I even asked! Just give me a sec, I'll put my walking boots on.'

We spend a few hours on the trails that wind through the forest. The heat is so intense we stop at a small stream, peel off our sweaty socks and paddle in the sun-sparkled water. Jasmine splashes me, her face lighting up with a cheeky grin, but she screams and runs away when I scoop up a great handful of water and chuck it at her.

There's a place I want to show Jasmine. We walk for about twenty minutes, our clothes drying rapidly in the late afternoon sun, shoes chafing against our damp feet. When we reach a small clearing, Jasmine stops and gasps, her eyes soaking up the carpet of buttercups, the way the sunshine bounces off their yellow petals. As we walk, dandelion heads rise up like a cloud of butterflies, tickling our faces and settling in our hair. Jasmine reaches out to try to catch them, laughing.

We sit down. The air is humming with insects and rich with the scent of grass, dry leaves and something delicate and floral that makes my nose itch.

Jasmine tells me about the time she tried to soften some butter in the microwave and the foil wrapper caught fire. I laugh drunkenly. The sun is making me woozy and I can't seem to stop. Jasmine joins in, threatening to give me a slap if I get hysterical. It only makes me laugh more.

'I love hearing you laugh,' she says. 'It's the only time I can imagine what your voice might sound like.'

We stay for a couple of hours, watching the sun arc across the sky in a dazzling haze. I am happy. So happy I feel like it should be radiating from me, as if my body can't contain it all. I'd be content to lie here for ever, just enjoying the sound of Jasmine's slow breaths, her closeness.

Eventually, we amble back to the campsite. Jasmine declares that she's starving, so we eat early, cooking up a pan of beans with rubbery cocktail sausages that bob up and down like buoys in a sea of tomato sauce.

We watch the sun set in a cloud-streaked sky that's tinted with shades of pale blue and light pink. Jasmine chats into the evening. Her words never seem to dry up. As soon as one sentence finishes, another springs up, bursting out with more energy than the last.

Sometimes I'll write her a question, ask about her life in Cyprus, whether she thinks Mr Finnigan looks a bit like Homer Simpson, or what she makes of this new boy band everyone's going crazy for.

Later, when the sky is doused with darkness, the moon appears, as pale and plump as a peeled Babybel. It sits low, almost stroking the treetops, its shadowy craters clearly visible. We spend a few silent moments just staring at it.

'Did you have a nice birthday?' Jasmine asks, her voice slurred with sleepiness.

I nod. *It was the best.*

Jasmine yawns. 'I can't stay up any longer. Shall we go to bed?'

I nod again and we crawl into the tent. I switch on the camping light. It chases away the shadows and fills the inside with a soft glow. There's a brief moment of awkwardness as we change into our pyjamas, each facing away from the other.

When Hana and I had sleepovers, we'd flick through girly magazines, get hyper on cherryade and Haribo, and giggle into the night, until one of our mums told us to 'settle down'. We'd make an effort to go to sleep, until one of us burst into laughter again and set the other one off.

Jasmine wriggles into her sleeping bag. I lie beside her, our faces inches apart, our breaths mingling. She coaxes the band from my ponytail, allowing my hair to spill across my shoulders, then she arranges it gently, stroking and smoothing it down. I close my eyes and try to control the quiver in my body.

'Your hair is lovely,' she whispers. 'Don't listen to your mum. Don't change it. I think it's gorgeous.'

I open my eyes and meet hers.

She doesn't look away. Breathes in. Out.

The air is trapped in my chest.

Jasmine takes another breath in, then out.

I can't move.

She inhales. Exhales. Calm and steady. Focused on me.

I'm hot. So hot my skin is crawling with it. Is she going to kiss me?

Her eyes are softening, her lips parting. I can't look away. I don't want to look away. I want her to kiss me, but if I move my head towards hers, if I'm wrong, I lose everything.

Jasmine moves her face a fraction closer.

She's going to do it! She's really going to kiss me!

Jasmine sighs and the air trembles from her lips. She blinks, says, '*Kaliníhta,* Megan *mou,* good night,' tucks a strand of hair behind my ear, and closes her eyes.

Cold disappointment floods through me. Tears shimmer in the corners of my eyes. I blink them away. I shouldn't let myself believe. Not even for a second.

I drag in some deep breaths, but it takes an age for my breathing to settle back to normal, for my heart to stop juddering. I watch Jasmine sink into sleep. I hadn't noticed before, but there are freckles on her nose, like a dusting of cocoa on frothy coffee. They're beautiful. Perfect.

Two words float up inside me. And tonight, there's no barrier. Nothing to stop them. 'Goodnight, Jasmine,' I whisper.

CHAPTER TWENTY-FIVE

I'm woken early in the morning by light pressing through our tent's thin canvas. It flickers over Jasmine's face, but she doesn't stir. I watch her for a few moments, fascinated by the way it highlights the shine on her dark eyelashes and reveals every crease of her lips.

After a few minutes, I wrench myself away and roll over. God knows what she'd think if she woke and caught me staring at her like that!

I settle for listening to her quiet snores, feeling the ebb and flow of her breaths on my neck, as regular as waves on a beach, surging back and forth, back and forth. The rhythm starts to lull me to sleep, until Jasmine groans, 'Megan? Are you awake?'

I turn, mouth clamped shut in case of morning breath.

Jasmine's eyes are still half closed. 'What time is it?'

I point to my watch.

'Six!' she croaks. 'Ergh. Remind me to bring an eye mask next time.'

I smile. Jasmine doesn't 'do' mornings.

The air in the tent is still and hot. I unzip the door. Jasmine complains, but her cheeks brighten when a rush of fresh air sweeps in. I rummage in my rucksack, knowing exactly what will wake her up.

'Marshmallows? For breakfast? Mum would kill me.' She grins. 'Let's do it!'

We scramble out and set up the stove. Jasmine lights it while I wander off, barefoot, in my pyjamas, to find a couple of twigs to use as skewers.

Jasmine is an expert at toasting marshmallows, leaving them in the flame until the skin starts to bubble and brown, then eating them quickly, before they cool. My attempts are less impressive and I end up with marshmallows that are either incinerated or barely warm. The sweet, slightly acrid scent of burnt sugar lingers around us, and it's not long before the ground is littered with globules of melted marshmallow.

The sugar rush goes straight to Jasmine's head and she gets the giggles. She points at me and laughs.

What? What is it? Have I got something on my face?

'You've got marshmallow goop on you.'

Jasmine tilts my chin up and lifts it off. It trails through the air like a spider's web, then she opens her mouth and pops it in.

Heat floods my skin. I look away, grabbing another marshmallow, even though I'm already queasy.

Inside the tent, Jasmine's phone starts to ring. Eleni. This will be her third call since we arrived. Jasmine disappears to root around for it.

'Hello? Yes, Mum, we're fine. Made it through the night without being murdered ... OK, calm down, I was only joking! Yes, we've got plenty of water ... No, you don't need to come now. We're staying for the rest of the day ... Why can't you just be relaxed about this, like Megan's mum? You're making a fuss ... Bye then.'

Jasmine emerges, grumbling.

I rub the top of her arm and she smiles and seems to relax. 'Shall we go for another walk today? I thought we could head off in the other direction?'

I nod and we start to get ready. Jasmine refuses to put her walking boots back on, claiming they're rubbing, and opts for canvas shoes instead. We smother ourselves in sun cream, load up our rucksacks and leave.

Even though it's only eleven o'clock, the heat is too much. We stop in the cool shade of the woods to eat lunch – a couple of squashed bread rolls and some blackened bananas.

'My heel is killing me,' Jasmine says. She prises off her shoe and reveals a massive blister. After examining it, she starts to hunt through her bag. 'I can't keep walking. I thought Mum put some plasters in here, but maybe I left them in the tent. Have you got any?'

I shake my head.

'Well, I'll have to go back. It's really painful. Why don't you carry on? We'll meet back at the campsite later.'

I shake my head again.

'OK. Sorry, Megan. I feel bad.'

By the time we arrive back at the site, we're both tired and sweaty, and Jasmine is walking with a slight limp. She lies on the grass outside the tent, hauling in gasps of hot air.

'Ice cream,' Jasmine mutters. 'I really want an ice cream. Or just some ice would be good. I'd pour a bucket of it over myself.'

I smile.

Jasmine doesn't say anything for so long, I wonder if she's fallen asleep, but when I glance over, her eyes are wide open.

I shuffle closer and point at her shoe. I want to have a look at the blister.

Jasmine squirms away. 'Really? You want to see? I'm warning you, Megan, it won't be pretty. I bet my foot reeks.'

But I insist and she takes it off. The blister has popped, the skin beneath it raw and red.

'Megan, you don't have to help. It's minging.'

But I want to. I find the plasters and use a wet wipe to try to clean around the wound. Eleni even thought to pack some anti septic cream and I dab it on, grimacing when Jasmine draws in a sharp breath.

I find the biggest, most padded plaster I can and carefully lay it over the top. I start to clean up, picking the plaster tabs out of the grass, but Jasmine reaches for my hand. 'Thanks,' she says.

Once again, she doesn't look away, but holds my gaze just a little too long. Maybe I didn't imagine it last night? Jasmine's hand is still on mine – it feels so good there – and she has the strangest expression on her face, which even I can't read.

Jasmine starts to speak, but her words trail off when we catch the sound of footsteps tromping through the grass.

I tense. Jasmine gasps and squints at the figure swaggering across the field towards us. 'It … it's Owen! I forgot I told him where we'd be.'

You did what? *This was supposed to be just us. I can't believe you did that!*

Jasmine is too busy scrabbling around for a hairbrush to notice how annoyed I am. I slip into the tent. It's almost unbearably hot. But I'm not going back out again. No way.

'Hi,' Jasmine says a few moments later.

Owen grunts a reply. 'All right?'

There's a metallic clicking sound. I'm not sure what it is, until I smell cigarette smoke. Owen must be flipping the lid of a lighter up and down. Does he really think that's impressive?

'Where's your mate?' he asks.

Click, click.

'In the tent. I think … Well, she's lying down. Not feeling too great.'

Liar. Why don't you just tell him that I don't like him?

'Want a fag?'

Click, click.

'No, thanks.'

'Wanna come for a walk?'

She can't go with him. She wouldn't.

'Er … I dunno. Can Megan come?'

'I came to see you.'

It sounds as if he starts to walk away, then Jasmine cries, 'No, wait!'

Please don't go off with him. I don't trust him.

You're just jealous.

'Well? You coming or what?'

'Yeah. All right.' Jasmine raises her voice, though she must know I can hear everything. 'Be back in a bit, Megan.'

Don't bother! You'd obviously rather spend time with your idiot boyfriend than me!

How could I think she had feelings for me? How could I be so stupid? I imagine Jasmine telling Owen, 'I think Megan's got a girl-crush on me. It's starting to get a bit weird.' I can see them laughing. My face burns.

I scrunch Jasmine's sleeping bag in my fists. Her scent wafts up from it. I let out a strangled scream and claw at the material, pulling and twisting until a rip opens in the lining. I chuck it out of the tent, followed by her pyjamas, her bag, and anything else I can find. Then I'm outside, wailing, kicking over the camp stove, flinging water bottles, lobbing pans across the field until my arms ache. I collapse in a shuddering heap.

That's when I realise what I've done. I let Jasmine go. I let her leave, knowing it was dangerous. I should've looked after her, just like I should've looked after Hana.

I tear off in the direction I think they went. I don't get far before I hear footsteps running towards me, and Owen's voice.

I can't hear Jasmine replying. He must be on the phone. I dart behind a cluster of trees and listen.

'Yeah, it's bad. Went up like a beast . . . Well, I left her, didn't I? It's her own fault if the silly cow thinks she can put out a fire on her own.'

Fire?

A forest fire?

OhmyGod. JASMINE!

CHAPTER TWENTY-SIX

I'm running.

Jasmine.

Feet pounding ground.

Please, Jasmine.

Left, then right.

Please don't be hurt.

Arms pumping.

I'm sorry.

Legs flying.

I should've gone with you.

Breaths gasping.

Why haven't you come back?

Blood rushing.

What if I'm too late?

*

Above the treeline, flames lick the sky. It's been days, weeks, since it rained. The whole forest – parched trees, dry bracken, brittle pinecones – is one great pile of kindling.

I reach the top of a small hill and see it all. My legs fold beneath me, my knees crunching on hard mud as I fall. The fire devours everything with an insatiable hunger. It crackles and spits, roars and hisses. Smoke gusts across the field, snagging in my throat.

Where is she? I can't see her!

Every sense is screaming at me to run away.

You're afraid. You don't have it in you.

SHUT UP!

I have to find Jasmine. I hurtle forward, clearing the field in seconds, then I plunge into the smoke.

My airway clogs. I try to drag in some clean air, but the smoke is too thick. Ripples of heat blast my skin. My eyes sting. Throat burns. I can hardly see.

Jasmine could be anywhere. How can I find her? Unless … My voice. But I can't. I can't just switch it on like that. My wind-pipe is almost blocked, my breaths grating in and out. I'm coughing so much I don't think I can stop. I can't. I'm sorry, Jasmine. I can't do it.

A memory shoots through me. The way Jasmine looked as she slept this morning, freckles dancing across her nose. Several more images crash into my mind: the look she gave me just half an hour ago, the way she touched my hair last night.

I can do this. For her. I try to shout, 'Jasmine!' but my voice is just a feeble croak. There's no response. I cough, then shout once more.

Against the thunderous bellow of the fire, I don't stand a chance.

My vision slides as I'm battered with waves of dizziness. I don't know where the ground is any more. I can't feel my feet on it. I'm floating. My legs give in. I sink down. Close my eyes.

'Help!'

I open them.

'Somebody help me!' Jasmine's voice is weak. In pain.

I sit up, start to crawl towards her. She's not far.

Keep shouting, Jasmine. Keep shouting! I'm coming.

'Somebody, please!'

I think I'm close, but her voice is quieter. Is she losing consciousness? I reach out, feeling blindly. But there's nothing but air. Where is she? I can't hear her any more! I can't see a thing. I've got ash in my eyes. God, it kills!

Then my fingers collide with something – her arm or leg – and I almost weep with relief. Is she breathing? My stomach twists. Please, let her be breathing. I can't lose her.

I rest my head against Jasmine's chest. It doesn't move. I cry out, clutch her face, let a few tears spill. More rise up, but I fight them down. I can't lose it now. *Come on, Jasmine.* Her chest rises, but only a little.

I shake her shoulders. Nothing. I try again, more vigorously, until Jasmine's head knocks against the ground. I slap her cheek, but I know I haven't hit her hard enough to bring her round. What the hell do I do? How am I going to move her? I tell myself not to panic, but the word is like a trigger, and suddenly there's a vice around my throat. I'm choking. I'm going to die here. We're both going to die here!

OK ... OK, stop it. Get a grip. I know what to do. I have to get Jasmine away from the smoke. Just the thought of it brings more tears to my eyes. I don't know if I have the strength to get myself out of this, let alone Jasmine. I'm not leaving her, though. I will not go through that again. I will not!

The fire is getting closer, its heat scorching my back. I need to move. Now.

I can't stand, but I can shuffle backwards on my knees. I hook my hands under Jasmine's arms. So heavy! Her head lolls sickeningly to the side. I drag her a couple of feet, then have to put her down. This is going to take ages. Too long! The fire is speeding towards us, engulfing everything in its path. But I grit my teeth and move her again.

Jasmine's lips are moving. Her eyelids quiver.

Jasmine! Don't pass out again.

I shake her, say her name. I lean towards her ear and say it again, louder.

But she's gone.

I haul her a few more feet, but I have to stop. I sit back on my knees, her head in my lap. My shoulders are aching, my arms trembling. I don't think I can pull her much further. I start to sob, my tears dropping on to Jasmine's still face.

I'm sorry. I'm so sorry.

A shaking, hot hand finds mine. Jasmine tilts her head back.

My eyes lock with hers. That look is all I need. I squeeze her hand, muster all the strength I have left, and stand, then heave Jasmine to her feet. I wrap one arm around her waist. Her body is limp and she leans heavily against me, but I won't let go.

We stagger away from the fire, one tiny step at a time. The smoke thins. I'm doubled over, wracked with coughs, but we're almost there. We push ourselves on, until the air is fresh and clear. I gulp it in, more grateful for it than anything in my life.

We collapse on our backs and lie there, filling our lungs between coughs. There's the distant wail of a siren.

'Megan?' Jasmine's voice is hoarse, tight with fear. 'Are you OK? Megan, please. Just nod or something.'

Am I OK? I don't know. I feel as if I've been gargling with shards of glass. My muscles are throbbing, my lips stinging, my chest sore, but I'm just about OK. I nod.

There are smudges of ash on Jasmine's face. Her hair is sticking up all over the place and her eyes are bloodshot and wild. 'God, Megan. You saved me! I can't believe you saved me. You were so brave.'

I wish I could tell her not to talk – she should rest. But telling Jasmine not to talk is like telling the fire not to burn. She coughs, then the rest of her words fall out in one great rush. 'I called the fire brigade. It happened so fast. I couldn't stop it. I tried to use a branch to smother the flames, but that caught light too and I burnt my hands.'

I wipe my watery eyes and look at her palms, which are a mess of red, seared skin. Before I can think, I lift myself up and kiss her fingers. Jasmine's lower lip drops. For a moment, we just stare at each other. The fire fades into the background. I forget how bad I feel, how every breath stretches my lungs tight.

Jasmine looks away. 'I'm sorry I left you.'

I shake my head. *We don't need to do this now. Just rest. We can talk later.*

But she's not looking at me. 'Owen and I had a fight. You were right about him. I was just so flattered that anyone would find me attractive. I—'

'You're beautiful,' I murmur.

Jasmine gasps, eyes wide with awe. 'What did you say?'

I open my mouth again. Nothing. But Jasmine is looking at me. Waiting.

Don't.

No. I'm sick of being a prisoner in my own body. It's my turn now. My time to speak.

'Say it again, Megan,' Jasmine whispers. 'I knew you'd find your voice. You're amazing. Say it again. I want to hear you speak.'

My jaw resists, but I force each syllable out. 'You're beautiful.'

It's hardly even a noise. My voice is husky, my pronunciation poor, but I know she understands.

Jasmine lunges forward and kisses me roughly, pushing hard to mould her mouth to mine.

My lips respond in an instant, brushing over the folds and furrows of her skin. There's a burst of warmth inside me and my hand winds through her hair, drawing her closer. She tastes of smoke and salty tears.

Jasmine is trembling. I wrap my arms around her, unwilling to break away for even a second. But it's her who ends it, jerking her head back. 'Megan,' she says, eyes pooling with tears as she touches her lips in disbelief. 'What are we doing?'

There's a shout behind us. A team of firemen jog through the grass. Three of them charge straight past like stampeding animals, the ground vibrating beneath their boots, while one stops to ask if we're all right.

For once, Jasmine has no words. Wrenching her gaze from mine, she nods.

'Is there anyone else in there?'

Jasmine is staring at the ground. I have to force myself to look at him and shake my head.

The fireman barks into a radio to request an ambulance.

As we wait for it to arrive, Jasmine is silent. She's pale, too. Whether it's shock from the fire, or from the kiss, I'm not sure. Her words bounce around my head like a solitary sock in a tumble dryer: *What are we doing?* I can still feel her lips, remember how she tasted, the way her body felt pressed against mine.

I knew what I was doing. Didn't she? Was she just caught up in it all? Did she only want to be comforted? Is she regretting it?

Whatever Jasmine's thinking, we can't go back now. Everything's changed.

*

The next few hours pass in a whirl of oxygen masks, stretchers and sirens. When I get to hospital, I'm whisked away for tests. I close my eyes and block it all out. An image of Jasmine's face is stamped on the back of my eyelids: that conflicted, stunned expression. It's all I see. All I think about.

In my cubicle, they turn on the TV and let me watch the news. It's taken hours, but after several helicopter dumps of water, the firemen have got it under control. They're not mentioning a cause yet. I wonder how much Jasmine will say. I remember Owen messing around with that lighter. Did he do it deliberately, to try to scare her? I wonder what they argued about. I wonder what she's thinking now.

I want to go home. I want to wrap myself in my own comfy duvet, not this clinical, scratchy thing. I want to smell Mum's coconut conditioner, instead of antiseptic. I want to get out of this horrible gown and put my bunny rabbit pyjamas on.

Apparently they've struggled to get hold of Mum. Her stupid mobile's always out of battery!

The nurses gently ask me questions. Jasmine must've given them my name when we arrived. They're puzzled by my lack of response, but don't press me. I hear one saying that it must be shock. I almost laugh. She doesn't know the half of it!

Not everyone is quite so understanding. In the early evening, my curtain is ripped open by a rotund policewoman with a crop of dark hairs hanging over her upper lip. At first, she is nice – smiling and asking how I am – but it's not long before she loses patience. Her bushy brows draw into a frown and she repeats the same questions over and over again.

'Playing dumb isn't going to help you, young lady.'

There are two specks of spittle rolling around the corners of her mouth. I can't stop watching them, terrified they're going to fly out and hit me in the face.

'All I want is the truth. We'll find out eventually, you know. The fire brigade have teams of investigators who can check these things. You've got nothing to gain by staying silent.'

Her interrogation is interrupted by a yell that echoes down the ward. 'Take your hands off me! I don't care if Jeremy bloody Kyle is interviewing her, I've told you, she won't say anything.'

Mum swipes back the curtain and glowers at the policewoman. 'You leave my daughter alone. She's not some hooligan who goes around starting fires. How dare you treat her like a suspect when she's lying there with an oxygen mask on?'

Another police officer – a wiry man with a dodgy tan and silver hair – steps forward and calmly tells Mum that, if she doesn't lower her voice, she'll be asked to leave. Mum harrumphs at this, but fixes the woman with a steely, mascara-rimmed stare. 'My daughter's a mute. If you don't believe me, check her GP records. It's all there.'

Moustache-woman pauses. 'Well,' she says crisply, 'I'll take a written statement.'

'Not until she's rested,' snaps Mum. 'Look at the state of her! She's exhausted.'

But the police officer insists, and I agree, just so Mum will stop making a scene. The policewoman hovers over me as I complete an official form, eyeing my every movement as if she's some kind of human lie detector. I don't mention that Owen was there. If Jasmine wants to drop him in it, it's up to her.

After it's done, and the police have left, Mum launches into a barrage of her own questions. How am I feeling? Too hot? Too cold? Does anything hurt? Do I know what happened? Did I see who started it?

I shrug. Not the response she's looking for, but I'm tired.

Mum tells me I look awful. She tries to say it with some sympathy, but it doesn't quite come out right. I look away. She heads off in search of coffee and chocolate, and probably a sneaky cigarette.

I listen to the news again, but they're just repeating the same information. They say the fire was reported by two campers. They don't give our names. I switch the TV off and catch whispered voices coming from behind the curtain. It's Mum and Eleni.

'I *knew* something like this would happen! We should never have let them go,' Eleni says. 'They could've been killed!'

'They're OK,' Mum replies. 'No point stressing about what might have happened.'

'Jasmine's barely said a word. I've never seen her like this. How's Megan?'

'It's hard to tell with her.'

'I'd better get back to Jasmine. Give Megan my love.'

Mum stays and chats to me for a while. A nurse pops in to tell us I won't have to stay overnight, which is a relief. Mum helps me get ready to go, but I pause and scribble a note to ask if she knows where Jasmine is.

We find her two cubicles down. She's staring straight ahead, into nothingness, responding to Eleni's questions in a monotone. When she notices I'm there, her eyes flick towards mine, then quickly move away.

Mum starts to walk towards Jasmine's bed, but I stop her, shaking my head and backing away. Mum frowns, but follows me out, shouting over her shoulder, 'Feel better soon, Jasmine.'

'Have you two had a fight?' she asks as soon as we're out of earshot. 'What happened?'

I shake my head. Mum sighs, then starts to rant about the cost of coffee at the hospital. I tune out. I can't shake that dull, dead expression on Jasmine's face. My eyes blur with unshed tears. She wants nothing to do with me.

You've ruined it. Just like you ruin everything.

CHAPTER TWENTY-SEVEN

Dear Jasmine,

I don't know where to start. My thoughts are all tangled and I can't find a beginning or end to them. So I'm sorry if what comes out is a mess. But I just need to get it out.

I can't stand not knowing what you're thinking. This last week has been horrible. Could you not have come to the door when I called for you? I just wanted to see you. I understand you're confused. If you want to talk, I'll listen.

If you think it was a mistake, you're wrong. If you think I was just caught up in the moment, I wasn't. It was real for me. I've wanted it for a long time. Everything changed when I met you. I've started to speak again, and I know you've played a big part in that. The truth is, when you kissed me, I think I was happier than I've ever been. I can't stop thinking about it. Or you.

I miss you so much. Will you come round this week? I won't push anything.

Please? Can we just try?

Megan xxx

CHAPTER TWENTY-EIGHT

The doorbell rings a couple of days after I deliver the letter. I'm still in bed, but I sit bolt upright, my heart hammering. Jasmine?

I hear the tap of Mum's heels as she goes to answer it. I scramble out of bed and fly to the top of the stairs. The door's opening. Mum's saying hello. Who is it? I can't see!

'No, thank you, we don't need any knives sharpening.'

Mum shuts the door firmly and stamps up the stairs. 'Bloody cheek, calling at this time! I'm going to be late for work. Have you seen my phone? I had it last night when I … Megan? What's wrong?'

I try to retreat to my room, but Mum grabs my arm and twists me round. I slump forward, nestling my neck in the crook of her shoulder. Mum's perfume catches in my throat as I breathe between sobs.

'Hey, what's all this about?' she asks. 'It's Jasmine, isn't it?

Look, whatever went on between you two, you'll sort it out. You'll be fine. Honest.'

I unwrap my arms, wipe the tears away.

Mum strokes my cheek. 'If you ever want to ...' I can almost hear her brain whirring as she searches for an alternative to 'talk', '... discuss anything, you know you can come to me, right?'

You wouldn't dare.

I shudder, swallow heavily.

'Megan? Did you hear what I said?'

I nod, give her a peck on the cheek. Then I lead her to the bathroom, where she left her phone last night.

Mum laughs. 'What's it doing there?'

I think she was bidding for something on eBay while she was shaving her legs.

Mum shakes her head. 'What am I like?' She ruffles my hair. 'What would I do without you?'

I shrug, wave goodbye, then head off to get ready. I'm going out for emergency chocolate supplies, then I plan on spending the rest of the day on the sofa.

I take the long route to the shop. Well, it's more of a detour, via Jasmine's house. I slow my steps as I walk past, eyeing the windows hopefully, but there's no sign of anyone. I imagine she's inside, just feet away from me. I wonder what she's doing now. I stay a few minutes, until I'm verging on stalker-territory, then I mooch off to the shop.

The moment I step through the door, I see Sadie, Lindsay

and Grace huddled around the magazines. Sadie is sniggering at some pictures of a drunken celebrity flashing her knickers. I start to back out. Too late. Sadie spots me and sidles over, Lindsay and Grace close behind.

'Megan Thomas. Aren't we just the talk of Brookby?' Sadie says, swiping a newly cut fringe from her eyes. 'Drama just seems to follow you, doesn't it?'

'You some kind of pyromaniac?' Lindsay asks.

'Megan didn't start it,' Grace says quietly. 'She was just there.'

'What do you know about it?' Sadie snaps. She turns back to me. 'So come on, Megan. Give us the gossip. Did someone start it deliberately?'

I shuffle backwards out of the door, colliding with someone behind me. I spin round, look up. Seriously? This just gets worse!

'Sorry,' Luke mutters, neatly sidestepping me.

My gaze sweeps down to the pavement. When I look up, he's gone, and his dad and Simon are following him inside.

'Hi, Megan!' Simon says through a mouthful of crisps. I manage a wave. Luke's dad says nothing. He's a big guy. Not just tall, but brawny, with a square head and two mean, squinty eyes.

I lean against the shop window. How did that just happen? The two people I least want to see, and they're both here! And the one person I do want to see has completely vanished. I need to leave. Sod the chocolate.

Sadie comes back out, tearing the wrapper off a packet of gum. 'You still here? Waiting for your boyfriend?' She braces her hands against the window, one each side of my head. I can smell the sickly cherry scent of her lip gloss. 'So what's the deal with Jasmine and Owen? I heard they broke up.'

Before I can stop myself, I glance up. *Really?*

'Shame. I guess she couldn't handle him. He's a bit of a live wire.'

Lindsay smirks.

Luke and his family emerge and head for a car parked against the pavement. Simon and Luke's dad get in, and Luke is about to when he glances up, sees us. He pauses, the door open. Then he walks over, shaking his head as if he knows it's a bad idea.

'Why don't you leave Megan alone?' he says to Sadie.

Lindsay eyes him coolly. 'That's none of your business.'

'I'm just saying ...'

Sadie whips round. 'What's your problem?' she snarls. 'I'm just talking to her.'

'Only because she doesn't talk back. Leave her alone.'

A glow of gratitude spreads through my stomach. *Thank you. You didn't have to do that.*

Luke's dad beeps the horn. Luke tenses, but doesn't look away.

'Why don't you piss off, Luke? Why are you sticking up for her anyway? Oh, I know!' Sadie draws a finger to her shiny lips, as if she's just had a revelation. 'It's because you have a massive crush on her. God knows why.'

Luke's face flares up. 'Evil cow,' he mutters.

The horn beeps again. 'Luke!' his dad bellows. Luke flinches.

I don't want him to go. I want to sort stuff out, make things better between us. It's bad enough that I've screwed up everything with Jasmine. I don't want to lose Luke as well.

But he can't stay. His dad is about to pop a vein or something.

'Run along now,' Sadie says. 'There's a good boy.'

Luke reaches the car in two quick, angry strides, wrenches the door open, then slams it behind him. Inside, his dad starts to yell, and the wheels screech as he pulls off and flies down the road.

Sadie yawns and stretches. 'Come on,' she says to Lindsay and Grace. 'It's boring here.'

I watch them leave, then let out a shaky sigh. Why did Luke do that? Why not let Sadie rip shreds out of me? Maybe he's not so angry any more. I should text him, say thanks.

I walk home with feet full of lead. There's so much pinging around my brain, I can't keep track of it all. A dull ache gathers around my temples, then spreads across the base of my skull, where it lingers for the rest of the day.

That night, Mum announces that she's going to call Eleni.

I pause, my fork halfway between the plate and my mouth. *Why?*

'I'm fed up of you slouching around the house, feeling sorry for yourself. This has gone on long enough. Whatever it is, you and Jasmine need to sort it out.'

I grab an old newspaper and write: *I've tried. I wrote her a letter and went round to see her. She doesn't want anything to do with me.*

'Well, that's not good enough! You can't give up. I lost a lot of mates when . . .'

When you had me, I think. *Go on, say it!*

'Well, I . . . I just wish I'd made more of an effort to keep them.'

I scrawl: *How is it that all* <u>*your*</u> *problems are* <u>*my*</u> *fault?*

'What are you on about? I didn't say that. I just don't want you to repeat my mistakes.'

What, I think, *like getting pregnant? Because that's the one mistake you'll never stop regretting.*

I push back my chair, glad to see Mum wince as it scrapes across the tiles.

'Megan!' she shouts as I storm away. 'She's the best friend you've had since . . . Look, I'm just saying, there aren't many people who would . . . this is all coming out wrong. Megan! Are you listening to me? She's worth fighting for.'

I know that.

But I don't know how else to fight. It's killing me that I can't fix this. I'm sick of trying to guess what's going through Jasmine's mind; tired of worrying that I've lost her for ever.

That's another friend you've driven away.
You're poison.

I write Mum a note to apologise, but ask her not to interfere. She grudgingly agrees not to call Eleni. I know she just wants to help. She wants me to be happy. I get that. But, right now, the only person who can make me happy doesn't want anything to do with me.

Things are a bit off between Mum and me for a couple of days. I know I've been acting like the stroppy teenager from hell. I decide to make her a cake. Baking's not really my thing, so I choose the simplest recipe I can find: a sponge. When it's all blended up, the mixture seems too runny. I check the cook-book and realise I've used one egg too many, so I add more sugar and flour.

It still seems too wet, so I shove it in the oven and increase the cooking time to dry it out. When Mum gets in, an hour later, I'm mixing up some icing to try to cover the burnt bits. She takes one look at me, with icing sugar peppered across my face and down my jeans; and the kitchen, which is a mess of broken eggshells and spilled flour, and bursts into laughter. It's not long before I join in, and we eat spoons of icing straight from the bowl until we feel sick.

Mum and I are languishing on the sofa in sugar-induced comas when the doorbell rings.

'You go, Megan. I can't be arsed,' Mum groans.

I shake my head. She knows I never answer the door to strangers.

'Go on,' she urges, nudging my leg with her toe.

I giggle and gently kick her away.

Mum huffs but gets up, grumbling as she shuffles to the door.

I mute the TV so I can listen. I hear the surprise in Mum's voice. My heart stops. Then beats again, really fast.

Jasmine.

I leap up and rush into the corridor, practically barging Mum out of the way.

Jasmine looks pale and stricken. Despite everything, all I want to do is wrap my arms around her.

'Can I come in?' she asks.

I nod, heat creeping up my neck, over my face. As we walk up the stairs, I glance back at Mum, who's watching us both with a soft smile.

In my room, Jasmine is stiff and formal. Worry draws her face into tight lines that weren't there before.

There's a weighty silence.

'How are you? I mean, apart from everything ...' Jasmine's words fall clumsily from her mouth.

Another silence.

'Bet you never thought you'd see me lost for words!'

Jasmine smiles, but she's on the brink of tears. Her mouth twists as she tries to hold them back.

After a few seconds, she gives in and starts to cry. I can't do anything but watch helplessly. I want to touch her, but what if she shrugs me off?

I can't bear it any more. I throw my arms around her. For a second, Jasmine tenses. I'm about to let her go, until she sinks into me, her body overrun with sobs.

I'm crying too. I don't know why Jasmine's here but, for the moment, I don't care. As long as I can hold her.

'I'm sorry,' Jasmine gasps. 'You must think I'm crazy, just turning up like this. I just ... I'm still so confused, but I've been miserable without you.'

I pull her close. Jasmine's scent makes me dizzy – that sweet, smoky incense. She strokes my hair, the back of my neck. Shivers shoot down my spine.

'Megan,' Jasmine mumbles. 'I've really missed you.'

My voice rises, desperate to escape, to tell her how I feel. Four words slip through my teeth. 'I missed you too,' I say in a dry whisper. The words taste wonderful, like chocolate melting in my mouth.

Jasmine smiles and starts to cry again. 'I love your voice,' she murmurs. 'I do have feelings for you, Megan, but I'm so messed up about the whole thing. The last person I ever want to hurt is you. And I don't want to ruin our friendship. I don't want to lose you.'

You won't lose me. I won't let that happen.

I pull away and gently hold Jasmine's face. Her lips are swollen, her nose red, but I still want her so badly. I move closer. Jasmine shuts her eyes. I feel the first, wonderful brush of her breath against my lips.

A floorboard creaks outside my room. Jasmine's head snaps round and she breaks away from me with a gasp. I turn to see what she's looking at.

This isn't happening.

My bedroom door is wide open.

Please, tell me this isn't happening.

Mum is standing in the corridor.

Did she see?

I look at her face.

She saw.

CHAPTER TWENTY-NINE

Mum drops the pile of washing she's carrying. I feel like it's happening in slow motion, like we're all plunging down with it, spinning through the air, until it hits the floor.

I drag my gaze from Mum and look at Jasmine, who is blushing furiously, a sheen of tears across her eyes.

No one speaks. No one breathes. No one moves.

Until Mum hauls her gaping mouth shut. 'Were you about to kiss her?' she asks me.

I want to shake my head, deny everything, but I just stare at her.

'Angela, Miss Thomas,' Jasmine says. 'I was just upset. Megan was comforting me.'

'No. She was going to kiss you. What's going on here? Are you two together? Is that why you haven't been round for ages? Because you broke up?'

'No!' Jasmine replies quickly. 'We kissed once. That was all, I swear. I don't really know . . . what this is. I don't think either of us do.'

I nod.

Mum kneels down and starts to pick the washing up, one piece at a time. She folds everything into little squares, even the socks, running her fingers along the edges to make sure they're folded properly. I throw Jasmine a horrified look. That's so not my mum!

Mum stands abruptly, says, 'Well, I'd better get this wash load on,' and hurries downstairs.

'Isn't it already clean?' Jasmine mouths.

I nod.

She gives me a sad smile. 'I'm going to go. Leave you two to talk.'

I nod again. I want to ask her to stay, to promise she'll come back, but she's right. I need to sort things out with Mum first.

After Jasmine has left, I sit on the edge of my bed and stare at the floor, trying to figure out what Mum's thinking. OK, she did just see me almost kiss a girl, which is bound to mess with her head a bit, but would she have a problem if I preferred girls to boys? *Do* I prefer girls to boys? Or is it just Jasmine? God, even I don't know!

I venture downstairs to make Mum a cup of tea. She's staring out of the kitchen window, playing with one of her hoop earrings. As I fill the kettle and find her favourite mug – the blue one with the bumblebees – she just watches me, saying nothing.

When the tea is ready, I press the mug into her hand and she takes it automatically, smiling and thanking me. She murmurs something about the wash, picks up her neatly folded pile, and heads for the utility room.

We eat microwaved roast dinners in front of the TV. The gravy is watery and over-salted. I let some of it drip through the prongs in my fork before taking a mouthful. Mum is picking at the meat and ignoring all the veg. She occasionally looks up at the TV, but she's not really watching it.

We both go to bed early, though it's obvious that neither of us will sleep. A few hours later, my mobile rings. No one ever rings me. But it's Jasmine, so I pick up.

'Don't worry,' she whispers. 'You don't have to say anything. I was just thinking that you might not be able to sleep.'

I smile into the phone. Just the sound of Jasmine's voice is like a sedative, creeping through me and soothing every angry, confused and frustrated thought.

'So I was wondering,' she says softly, 'if I could just talk to you for a bit? And maybe it'll help. If you don't want me to, just hang up. I won't be offended, I promise.'

I snuggle into my pillow and prop the phone against my ear as Jasmine starts to tell me about the pine forests in Cyprus and the mountain trails that meander through them. There's a riverside walk which ends in a waterfall, and it's so isolated you can strip off to your underwear and stand beneath it.

When I wake the next morning, I can't remember anything else Jasmine said. I must've fallen asleep after a few minutes.

Mum's already in the kitchen when I come down. She chats

a bit about work, but she's still quite subdued. I chuck some cereal in a bowl and shovel it down so I can escape upstairs. Ten minutes later, Mum leaves for work, early for once.

She couldn't stand to be around you any longer.

I'm not sure if Jasmine will come today, but when I glance out of the window, I see her hovering in the street outside. She seems to be a bit apprehensive about ringing the doorbell. But as soon as I go out, her face relaxes. 'Was it OK, what I did last night?' she asks.

I grin. *It was more than OK. It was the nicest thing anyone's ever done for me. God, I wish I had the words.*

I squeeze her hand – I love feeling her skin against mine – and hope she understands.

Jasmine catches me up on everything that's happened since the fire. I'm listening, but my mind is full of other stuff, like how to figure out what's going on between us, or what I'm going to do about Mum. But when Jasmine starts talking about the fire, I snap to attention.

'They still haven't found who started it. It's really creeping me out, Megan. Someone has it in for me.'

I frown and write: *What do you mean? I thought it was Owen. He was mucking around with that lighter.*

Jasmine gasps, then grabs my arm. 'I didn't tell you! I saw someone running away. It wasn't Owen. He was with me when the fire started.'

What?

'And someone trashed our campsite. Didn't Mum mention it when she dropped your stuff off? They ripped my sleeping bag. Left another note inside.'

What's she saying? It was me who wrecked the campsite, tore the sleeping bag. But I didn't leave a note ... did I? Am I actually losing my mind? No. It's not me. It can't be. I would know. I would remember. As if I could kill a cat, start a forest fire. That's ridiculous.

Is it?

'The police are taking the notes seriously now. They're checking them for fingerprints, or whatever it is they do.'

What the hell are they going to find? It can't be me. It can't be.

Are you sure?

'Anyway, as soon as the fire started, Owen did a runner. Said he'd almost been done for arson a couple of years ago, and that the police would pin it on him. So he just left me. What a bastard! We're definitely over.'

Definitely over. Thank God for that. At least something good has come out of all this. But still ... someone deliberately started that fire and I know it wasn't me. I glance at Jasmine. Nobody's going to hurt her. Nobody.

*

Jasmine and I pop over to hers to watch a DVD in the afternoon. When I get home, Mum is waiting for me. 'Hello,' she says, standing in the doorframe and wringing her hands. 'Can we talk? I mean ... you know what I mean.'

I follow her to the kitchen and lower myself into a chair, heart thudding. I pick up a pen and watch as it twirls through my fingers like a baton. I feel like they're someone else's fingers.

Mum pulls out a chair opposite me. She pauses for a long moment, then asks quietly, 'How long has this thing with Jasmine been going on?'

I write: *It isn't really a thing. I don't know. We kissed after the fire. But I've been having feelings for her for a while.*

'How could you not tell me?'

Mum's eyes are all red and she's covering her mouth with her hand.

I didn't know how to, I start to scribble.

Mum interrupts. 'Do you talk to her?'

I give her a questioning look.

'I bet you do, don't you? I bet you talk to her all the time. I'm your mum, Megan, but you trust her more than you trust me.' Her voice breaks. 'You've been going through ... all this ... and I didn't even know. I don't know you, Megan. I feel like I don't know you!'

I struggle with the apple-sized lump in my throat. *Is that why you're upset?* I write. *Not because I was going to kiss a girl?*

Mum swats it away as if it's nothing. 'I don't care about that!' she cries. 'I mean, I'll admit it was a bit of a shock. I'm still getting my head around it, but I don't care. Not really. I don't know if this is just a phase, but it's fine if you want to, you know, experiment, find yourself, or whatever. I just can't believe I didn't know how you were feeling! I should've known.'

I reach for her hand, but she pulls away.

'So do you talk to Jasmine?'

I look her in the eyes, then I write: *I've said a couple of things to her.*

Mum nods. She tries to hide how hurt she is, but she lets out a massive sob. 'I try my best, Megan. I know I'm a bit of a mess. I'm a lot of things, but I'm still your mum. And I don't get why you can't just open up to me. I was hoping things would be better between us after Grandpa died. I thought you might … I don't know, turn to me instead.'

My heart crumples like a crushed can. I had no idea she felt like that. I kick back my chair to rush over and throw my arms around her, holding tight.

'I love you, Mum,' I murmur.

The colour leaves her face and, for a moment, it's her who's speechless. Mum swallows, then says in a croaky voice, 'I love you too, so much.'

We spend a good ten minutes crying into each other's arms, until my stomach rumbles loudly.

Mum swipes mascara streaks from her face. 'Let's have a takeaway for dinner. Treat ourselves!'

I nod and go off to find a menu, leaving her to repair her make-up.

*

A couple of days later, Jasmine has an announcement to make. 'We've booked a last-minute holiday to Cyprus,' she says, 'and we want you to come!'

'Me? Go to Cyprus? When?'

'On the day the exam results come out.'

I leap forward, clutching her in a tight hug.

Jasmine gives me an impulsive kiss. Then her eyes soften and her movements become more slow and gentle, almost shy, as she kisses me again.

Afterwards, Jasmine starts to gush about what we're going to do in Cyprus. I've noticed that, as I've started to speak more, Jasmine has got better at listening, and not talking so much herself. But I let her get away with it this time, because it's just so adorable.

'It's going to be amazing, Megan. I've already planned where I'm going to take you. There's this awesome taverna in the mountains where they do an incredible mezze. The best in Cyprus! Just when you think you can't eat any more, they bring out a plate of chips. They're gorgeous. All greasy and soft and freshly cooked.'

My mouth waters. A year ago, I wouldn't have imagined I'd be brave enough to go to Cyprus, but one look at Jasmine and I know I'd follow her anywhere.

I ask Mum as soon as she gets home. She's glancing over a pile of letters, but stops to look up at me. I catch a flicker of jealousy before she hides it and smiles. 'Course you can, you lucky cow!'

Her eyes flit down to a bank statement and her mouth

pinches. 'As long as you're happy to use some of the money that Grandpa left you?'

I throw myself at her and she sort of gasps and laughs at the same time. 'We'll need to get you ready. You'll definitely need a pedicure if you're going to be sunbathing. Do you even own a bikini? You'll need to get everything waxed.'

I snort. As if!

I start to go upstairs.

'Hang on a minute,' Mum says, thrusting something at me. 'This one's for you.'

I open it in my room. It's from the photography competition organisers. My hands shake as I skim the letter. All I see are the words 'regret to inform you'. Damn. I haven't won.

I give it a second, more thorough read and realise I've been 'highly commended' for the picture of Jasmine I submitted to the 'Humans and Nature' category. It's been posted on their website.

I charge into the spare room and switch on our archaic computer, drumming my fingers against the mouse as it boots up. When I finally get the website to load, I flick through the shots until I find my picture: a close-up of Jasmine, her hazel eyes reflecting silhouettes of the trees above.

I copy the link and email it to her, with the subject line: *You're stunning*. I imagine her reaction – the way she'll blush, then do that lovely half-smile thing she does. I think Jasmine might be starting to believe me. I pay her compliments all the time, and stop her when she pulls faces at herself in the mirror.

I bound downstairs and lead Mum up to the computer. 'Oh

my God!' she shrieks, jumping up and down like a child on a trampoline. 'It's your photo!'

We have a few mad moments of dancing around, until Mum collapses on her bed, declaring that she's 'too old' for all this.

I'll be starting sixth form in three weeks. Three weeks! How am I going to deal with a new place? With all those people who don't know that I can't speak? Why do I have to make things harder on myself? I should've stuck with Barcham Green. Then at least I'd be moving up with Jasmine.

Things are good between us. We've been stealing kisses here and there. Something has awoken and expanded inside me, like the leaves of a fern uncoiling from a tight spiral. I don't think I'll ever get used to it. Neither of us is sure what 'it' is yet, but that's OK.

I've been delaying telling Jasmine the truth about Hana. Tomorrow, I think. I'll tell her tomorrow. But every day we spend together, we grow closer, and that just makes it more difficult. How's she going to feel about me when she knows who I really am?

I can't keep finding excuses, though. Jasmine deserves to know everything, before 'it' becomes something else, something more.

I need to do it for me, too. Mr Harwell is right. I have to break down that dam, even though I'm scared that I'll lose myself if I let it all back in.

In the end, it's the date that decides for me. The eighteenth of August. The day my life was fractured into pieces, and I lost parts of myself I never recovered.

Jasmine and I are lounging in my back garden, our hands linked.

'We need to talk,' I say.

Keep your mouth shut.

Jasmine sits up. 'What about?'

Leave it alone.

Please, just let me get the words out.

NO! DON'T YOU DARE!

'Megan, what is it? What's the matter?'

DON'T TELL ANYONE.

'It's been exactly a year since Hana died.'

BITCH!

'Oh, Megan. I'm so sorry. You poor thing. You should've said earlier.'

'There's more.' Hot tears chase each other down my cheeks as I force each word out. 'Hana's death. It . . . it was my fault.'

MURDERER.

Jasmine drops my hand.'It was just an accident, Megan. I get why you blame yourself, but it honestly wasn't your fault.'

'No. I killed her. I damaged the rope on the swing.'

YOU'RE FINISHED.

Jasmine stands abruptly, almost tripping over her own feet. 'What?'

'I killed her,' I repeat.

'Megan, you're not making any sense.'

'I'll tell you. Just sit down.'

'Sit down? No. You can't . . . you can't just dump something like that on me! You've just told me that you killed . . . I can't . . . you killed someone? Your best friend. I . . . don't . . . I don't know . . . Who the hell are you, Megan?'

I scramble up.'I can explain, I swear. Just stay. Please.' I gently touch her hand, but she flinches as if I've burned her.

'Don't.' Jasmine's voice almost cracks; her eyes are blazing. 'If . . . if you're saying you're capable of that . . . What else, Megan?'

I can barely stand to look at her, to see that beautiful face clouded by suspicion. I reach for her once more.'Just listen—'

'No.' Jasmine shakes her head, backing away.'I can't do this.'

She spins on her heel and charges out of the garden. I call after her, begging her to stay, but she's gone.

What have I done?

CHAPTER THIRTY

It started with a text. I remember everything about the day Hana got that text, from the catkin-shaped rust patch she'd noticed on her bike in the morning, to the hot heaviness in the air as I waited for her outside the shop.

Hana bounded out, without the promised Maltesers or Cokes, her eyes bright. 'Look what I've got!' she said, waving her phone in front of me.

I frowned, trying to focus on the moving blur. 'What? What is it?'

'A text!'

'From who?'

'Grace.'

My stomach scrunched into knots. 'What does she want?'

'She's inviting me to a party at the ridge on Saturday.'

'Why does she suddenly want to be friends again?'

'I dunno. But we can both go.'

'I don't think so!'

Hana looked shocked, then a little hurt. 'Why not?'

'It's obvious why not!'

She stared at me blankly, so I said, 'It's some nasty joke. They're just inviting you to take the piss.'

Hana fixed me with her best glare. 'You're just jealous.'

I snorted. 'I don't care. Do you seriously want to hang around with them?'

'Maybe I've grown up.'

I shot her a sharp look. 'And I haven't?'

'I didn't say that. Look, this is stupid. Why don't you come along?'

'No. They asked you, not me.'

'Don't be like that. Come on, Megan, why don't you try something new for a change? Don't be such a wuss!'

Hana strutted around, sticking out her neck and flapping her arms like wings. I pretended to ignore her, until she started making clucking noises, then I slapped her lightly on the arm, laughing. 'I'm not a chicken. I can do crazy stuff.'

'Yeah, right!'

I shrugged. 'Whatever.'

'Look, if it goes well, and I get to sit with them at school, I'll make sure you get invited over. Promise.'

'What, to sit with Sadie?'

'God, she's not that bad!'

'Apparently not, seeing as you're so desperate to become one of her Barbie clones.'

There was silence as we both tried to stare the other down. My cheeks felt crimson and Hana's eye was doing that weird twitchy thing it did when she was wound up.

I sighed. 'Just do what you like. It's fine.'

'It's not though, is it? I want you to come, but I'll go on my own if I have to.'

'As if your parents will let you!'

'I'll work something out. Tell them I'm at yours. They won't find out.'

'They will if I tell them.' It was cruel, but I was willing to throw anything at Hana to stop her from making such a massive mistake.

Hana gasped. 'Don't you dare! Don't even think about it, Megan. If you do, I'll never speak to you again, I swear.'

'Well, if you go to the ridge on Saturday, I'll never speak to *you* again.'

Hana took a deep, shaky breath, but didn't release it. I watched her, transfixed. It felt like everything was hanging on that breath. She was wavering. But then her eyes hardened and I knew she'd made up her mind. I wanted to walk away, cover her mouth, anything to stop her from speaking.

'I'm sorry, Megan,' she said in a sad, soft voice. She got on her bike and, without a backward glance, cycled away.

I watched until she was just a tiny, Hana-shaped speck at the end of the road, then she swung round the corner by the Post Office and was gone.

I knew what would happen next. Sadie would poison Hana, turn her against me. I was going to lose my best friend: the only person who hadn't laughed when I slipped on a sanitary towel wrapper on the first day of Year 7 and fell flat on my back; who made me giggle when she put cherry tomatoes in her cheeks and slapped them so hard the juice squirted out of her mouth; who missed a sci-fi convention she'd been raving about for weeks so she could stay with me on the day I found out Grandpa had cancer.

How would I manage without her?

I couldn't get out of bed the next morning. Not until I'd decided what to do. Did I give Hana more time to figure out what she wanted? She must've known she'd have to change to fit in with them. Wouldn't she realise it wasn't worth it, just to be popular?

I had to try one more time. I marched over to Hana's house, firming up my argument in my mind, rehearsing what I was going to say. But when I got to the front door, I hesitated. What if I made things worse?

No. She was my best friend. I wasn't giving up without a fight. I rang the bell, my chest squeezing. After several, quick heartbeats, the door opened. I instantly searched Hana's face as I tried to figure out if she was still mad.

She gave me a brief smile. 'Have you changed your mind? Are you coming now?'

'No. I was going to try to change *your* mind.'

The smile dropped straight away. 'Well, you might as well

not have bothered. I'm allowed to have other friends, Megan.'

'But your choice in other friends is crap.'

Hana scowled. I'd never seen her look so scathing. 'You're being a total bitch, you know that?'

I did. Part of me did. But I still couldn't stop myself.

'*I'm* the bitch? You're the one who's betraying her best friend!'

'You're overreacting. You should leave.'

She tried to slam the door in my face. I put my foot out to stop it and it bounced back, straight into her hand.

Hana screamed. 'God! What's your problem?'

I felt sick. 'I'm sorry. I didn't mean to …'

'Shut up! I don't want to hear it. Leave me alone.'

'Fine.'

But it wasn't fine. Not at all. There was an even bigger wedge between us. Hana was making it so easy for Sadie to swoop in and tear us apart. Why was she letting this happen? Did our friendship mean so little to her?

I went straight to the only other person I could talk to. Luke. 'Screw Hana,' he said. 'If she wants to go off with Sadie, let her. Why don't we have our own party? We can have fun without her.'

I wasn't sure. It didn't sound like much of a party if it was just Luke and me. But what else was I going to do? Just sit around at home, stewing about Hana?

Luke and I met in the forest at night. Years ago, Owen's dad had built this swing – a circle of wood with a hole through the middle for a rope – and hung it on a tree above a river. Everyone knew that only Owen and his mates got to use it. Anyone else would be in serious trouble if they were caught.

It didn't worry Luke that night, though. 'Owen's a tosser,' he said, slopping his beer everywhere as he clambered on to the swing. 'I dunno what you all see in him.' He put on a high-pitched, girly voice: '*Owen's so hot! He's well fit. Have you seen his abs?*'

I giggled. 'I don't get it either. He's nothing special.' I took another swig of Lambrini. It was gross. I almost couldn't swallow it, but I made myself. I'd show Hana.

An almost-full moon poked through the trees as Luke swung over the water, his face dappled with the shadows of leaves. Someone had tied a strip of glow-in-the-dark material around the rope, like those dorky things cyclists wear around their ankles, and it gleamed yellow in the darkness.

'I can't believe Hana's going off with them,' I said.

'I tell you what we should do,' Luke replied, with a laugh. 'We should mess with Owen's precious swing. I'm not scared of him.'

I frowned. I thought we were talking about Hana?

Luke pulled a penknife from his pocket. It flashed in the moonlight as he drew out one of the blades.

My gut clenched. I suddenly felt very cold. What was he doing with that?

Luke had stopped swinging and was just swaying slightly in the breeze, his eyes fixed on the blade. 'We could fray the rope here, see?' he said quietly, almost to himself. 'The wood will cover it so no one will notice. The next time someone sits on it, the rope will snap and they'll fall straight into the water.' He threw his head back and laughed.

I took a step away and smiled uncertainly.

'What do you reckon?' he asked.

I wondered if Hana would be the next person to use the swing. If she got in with Sadie's gang, she'd be allowed to use it. I pictured her face as she clambered out of the river, sopping wet, while Sadie and her mates cracked up. My cheeks flushed, instinctively feeling her shame. That was how it had always been with Hana – I felt everything that she felt. Then I reminded myself that she was turning her back on me, that soon she wouldn't think twice about laughing when Sadie called me a freak or a loser.

'I hope it's Hana,' I spat. 'Would serve her right.'

'Here you go.' Luke slipped the blade back in and lobbed the penknife towards me. It landed in the dirt by my feet. I picked it up, felt the solid weight of it in my palm, and curled my fingers around it.

'Luke?'

'Yeah.'

'What's going on with you and Hana?'

'Don't worry about it, Megan. Stop thinking about her. You should drink more.'

Should I? I already felt pretty pissed. I'd made my point: that I wasn't as boring as Hana thought, that I could be just as fun as Sadie. But Hana's words were still ringing around my head. *Leave me alone. You're being a total bitch. Don't be such a wuss! You're just jealous.*

I took Luke's advice. I drank more. A lot more. So much that I don't really remember the rest of the evening.

On the night of Sadie's party, I did what any self-respecting best friend would do: I gatecrashed. I waited until it was dark, then cycled over to one of the car parks. There were bikes strewn across the gravel and music and laughter floated across on the warm summer breeze.

It was a ten-minute walk to the ridge. I turned the torch off when I got close. I fumbled around in the dark, tripped once, and tried not to swear too loudly.

I lingered in the shadows, watching. The moon lit everything up like a giant spotlight. Hana was there, plus Sadie, Grace, Lindsay, Josh and Ben. The girls were drinking bright blue alcopops and the ground was littered with the boys' beer cans. A mobile phone was hooked up to some speakers and was blasting out a dance track. A couple of camping lights attracted a cluster of determined moths.

Hana stood at the edge of the group, hands shoved in her pockets, shoulders up by her ears. Grace was next to her, chatting, swaying her hips to the music.

'Let's do dares!' Sadie shouted. 'I'll go first. What do you dare me to do?'

'Flash us your bra!' Josh yelled.

Sadie ignored him.

'Spit into the ridge!' Ben said.

Sadie took a mouthful of drink, tottered to the edge, and

leaned forward. I heard her spit, then she started to giggle. She wiped her mouth. 'Hana, you're next.'

Hana shot nervous glances from face to face. 'Um ... OK.'

Sadie threw her arm around Josh. 'Gotta be something hard, to prove you really want to hang around with us.'

She's going to do something stupid. Dangerous. 'No way,' I breathed, breaking my cover to rush up to them.

Sadie was the first to see me. She curled her lip. 'Who invited *you*?'

'Megan?' Hana asked.

Sadie rounded on her. 'Did you invite her?'

'Please don't do this,' I said to Hana. 'You don't have to prove anything to them.'

Hana looked at Sadie, then back at me. She blushed.

I couldn't believe it! She was ashamed of me. Tears burned my eyes. Everyone was glaring at me.

Hana broke the stony silence. 'Go home, Megan.'

'Fine,' I snapped. 'I'm done with you.'

I stamped down the hill. I refused to blink and let the tears fall. She would *not* make me cry. When I was sure they couldn't see me any more, I turned to look back at them.

There was an old tree clinging to the edge of the ridge, its branches sweeping into the black nothingness above the drop. Someone had tied a rope swing to it, and Ben was helping Hana get on the seat.

Ben let go and Hana squealed as the swing arced through the air. She stretched her legs out and flung her head towards the sky. 'Wheeee! This is so much fun!'

I watched her swoop through the night. She looked so free, so happy. I envied her. I wished I were as brave as her. The only swing I'd dare to go on was the ...

Everything inside me turned to ice. No. It couldn't be the same swing. There must be two of them. But it looked the same. It looked the same! Had Luke and I done something to that swing? We'd talked about it, but what had we done? I couldn't remember. Why couldn't I remember?

I took a few steps towards Hana. My foot scuffed something. I looked down. Oh no. Please, please, please, no. There was a strip of glow-in-the-dark material lying on the ground.

'Hana!' I cried, running forward.

But she couldn't hear me. She was shrieking and whooping as she glided through the air. The rope snapped. And suddenly my best friend wasn't there any more. She didn't scream. She didn't even have time to scream. There was a devastating crack as her body hit the ground. It echoed through the forest, again and again and again, or was it just echoing through my mind?

It was my fault. I did that. I frayed the rope. I must have frayed the rope. Luke gave me the penknife. What did I do? I killed her!

There was screaming. A lot. Mine. Other people's. It all merged into one. There was crying, people yelling at each other. A phone call to the police. And pain. So much pain I thought I'd never cry it out.

Someone dragged me to my feet, their fingers digging into my arms. I didn't even remember falling. They were shaking me, shouting. It was Sadie. I couldn't understand anything she was saying, though. There was this voice in my head. It was so loud it cut through everything else.

It's your fault. You did this.

I was sick on Sadie's shoes. Her stupid, expensive shoes.

We heard sirens, then everyone started throwing cans and bottles into the bushes.

There were lights. Flashing, coloured ones. Flickering torch beams. Bright white ones that shone in my face, exposing my secret, revealing my guilt.

A policewoman crouched beside me and draped a blanket over my shoulders. 'You poor thing,' she said in a soothing voice. 'Can you tell me what happened?'

I opened my mouth, but the words huddled inside, terrified, trapped.

They thought it was shock. 'Her voice will come back,' they reassured Mum. 'Give her time.'

But there was nothing.

The police took a written statement from me. I told them that Hana had done it as a dare, that she'd been showing off. I kept everything else locked inside, along with my voice.

The pain still steals my breath away. I struggle for a few moments, almost hyperventilating.

My phone buzzes. Jasmine! But it's from a number I don't recognise. I stare at the words. They're fluttering around like insects, not settling anywhere.

You told her! I tried to warn her off, but you've ruined everything. She can't be allowed to talk.

I call the number straight back, but there's no answer.

Who the hell is this from? What do they think I've told Jasmine?

My hands are shaking so much I can barely use my phone. Come on! Faster! Eventually, it starts to ring Jasmine. *Please, pick up. Don't ignore me.*

'What do you want, Megan?' Her voice is clipped, cold.

'Jasmine! Where are you?'

She doesn't answer straight away, as if she's afraid to tell me exactly where she is. Then she says, 'At the ridge.'

'You need to leave. You're in—'

'Look. I've got to go. Luke's here.'

'JASMINE!'

But she's already hung up.

Luke? Why is Luke there? What's going on? If Luke's with her, does that mean ... he's the one who sent that text? She must've told him what I said about Hana. But it can't be Luke. The message sounded so sinister, threatening. What does *She can't be allowed to talk* mean? What's he going to do to her?

My hands are slick with sweat as I hit redial. It rings and rings. No answer. I try again. Straight to voicemail.

She's turned her phone off.

I'm going to lose everything again.

CHAPTER THIRTY-ONE

When I get to the car park, there's only one bike there: Luke's. He must've given Jasmine a backie. God knows how he persuaded her to go with him!

I charge up the path that leads to the ridge, my legs trembling from the furious bike ride, my heart slamming, its beat thumping through my ears. The path is lined with stinging nettles, but I barely feel their prickle against my ankles.

I stare at the text again, searching for any clues that it really did come from Luke. It's not his number. But didn't he say something about getting a new number?

I tried to warn her off. So was it him sending the ... But how could it be? How could the same guy who held my hand in the cinema be capable of those disgusting notes? The cat? The fire? This is the boy I've known since I was five. I just can't connect it all. No. It can't be him. I'm going to get there and he'll explain everything, and I'll be embarrassed for doubting him.

But there he is, at the top of the ridge, bellowing a stream of hate into Jasmine's face. And everything I thought I knew dissolves within me. Jasmine has her back to the deadly drop, and she's trying to inch away from Luke, but she's getting closer and closer to the edge.

Why does he want to hurt Jasmine? Why is he so angry? I've never seen anyone so mad. He's quivering with rage. His muscles are taut, his skin red. How could I not have known he was like this? I let him kiss me! And now I've put Jasmine in danger.

I try to move, but it's like my legs have grown roots. Jasmine throws a glance over her shoulder, down into the ridge, and when she looks back, everything about her screams fear, from her horrified, bulging eyes to her colourless, clammy skin.

'Get away from me!' She raises her hands to try to push him away, but Luke is faster and grabs Jasmine's wrists. 'You couldn't have just left Megan alone!' he's yelling. 'Do you see what you've done?'

They start to grapple. Move, Megan, move! Do something! Don't let her die like you let Hana die.

For a moment, it looks like Jasmine is winning, but then she loses her footing and stumbles back a couple of steps. She's going to fall! My legs unlock and I fly forward. I try to shout, but there's nothing except a guttural noise at the back of my throat. I try again, forcing the words out, beyond the blockade: 'Luke, stop!'

Luke whips round. His mouth drops. 'Y-you're talking.' He flips back to Jasmine, shakes her, flecks her face with spit as he yells, 'I knew this would happen! This is because of you. All because of you. Now she'll tell everyone.'

Luke doesn't let go of Jasmine, but looks back at me. 'We agreed to keep it a secret,' he snarls. 'You promised!'

I nod, remembering the state Luke was in when he came to my house the day after Hana's death. As soon as he said we had to keep it between ourselves, I knew I'd sabotaged that rope. But Luke was going to protect me, keep my secret.

'What did you tell her, Megan? She said you told her the truth about Hana. What exactly did you tell her?'

Nothing, I want to say. But my tongue seems to swell. The words are choking me.

'She didn't say anything, Luke!' Jasmine shrieks. 'She just said it was her fault that Hana died.'

Luke frowns. 'Her fault? What are you talking about?' He turns on me. 'Why are you lying?'

I shake my head. I'm not. We both know it was my fault.

'I tried to stop this, Megan. I knew it would happen if you got close to someone. Knew you'd start to blab. I've seen the way you look at her.'

When he looks at Jasmine, Luke's face is contorted with hatred.

Jasmine's so close to the edge, the back of her shoe keeps slipping, dislodging pieces of the verge.

I run at Luke, try to wrestle him away, but he pushes me back with one hand. His eyes are bloodshot, almost feral.

'I sent the notes because I wanted her to leave you alone. But she didn't listen. I had to make her listen. Don't you see? Then you told me her parents had moved house to protect their precious princess from being bullied.'

I swallow heavily. Why had I told him that? I shouldn't have told him.

'I thought if things got more serious, they'd move again. Leave us alone. And things could go back to the way they were before. I liked you, Megan. Just like I liked Hana.'

Drops of sweat are gathering at Luke's temples, slicking his messed-up hair to his face. 'And now I don't know what to do,' he says softly.

Jasmine's literally teetering on the edge. Luke is the only thing stopping her from plummeting over. 'What do I do?' he screams at her.

'Let me go! Just let me go!' she wails.

'But it's gone too far,' he mutters. 'She knows too much.'

'Megan!' Jasmine screams.

I lunge forward, grab Jasmine's sleeve, try to pull her towards me. Luke lets go of Jasmine and wrenches my hand away. Then I realise – to my horror – that neither of us is holding her.

Jasmine pitches backwards, arms flailing.

'No!' I gasp, reaching out.

But I'm too late.

She's gone.

I sink down. There's this tiny, bald patch of earth by my knees. The dry dirt crumbles beneath my trembling touch. Its scent rises up: earth, dust, death.

She can't be gone.

She is. She's gone.

But she died thinking I'm a killer. I never got to explain.

Now she'll never know. And I'll never touch her again, kiss her, feel the smooth skin of her hand wrapped around mine, tuck one of her curls behind her ear, curve my arm around her waist and draw her towards me, where she belongs.

Belonged.

No. God, Jasmine, no!

I rake my fingers through the dirt, barely aware of what I'm doing. I'm losing myself. I can't hold on. There's nothing left but a surge of grief, guilt, anguish, anger, fear. The dam has broken. I'm flooded with it all, tossed around like a fishing boat in a mighty storm. It's tearing me to pieces. I'm breaking, shattering, splintering.

Someone's calling out to me. A tiny voice. 'Megan!'

I open my eyes.

'Megan, help!'

Jasmine? I peer over the edge, release something that's half-laugh, half-cry. Jasmine! She's there! I can see her!

She's fallen about ten metres down the slope. Her body has been caught by a bush, but it's not going to hold her for long. Some of the roots have already been pulled out of the ground, and it's leaning dangerously to the side. Once it gives, there will be nothing to stop her from crashing to the bottom.

'Megan, help!' Jasmine cries. 'My ankle. It's killing me!'

Behind me, Luke's crouched low to the ground, cradling his head in his hands, convulsing with sobs.

I shake the fug from my head, think quickly. The ridge is so, so steep. The only way to reach Jasmine is to slide on my stomach.

I start to wriggle down. With my chest pressed against the ground, I can barely breathe. My palms scratch against stones and twigs. I can taste soil and sweat, but I don't care. I can see her. She's alive.

Jasmine moans with relief when I reach her. I grab her, pull her to me, kissing her face, her hair, her neck. I trail my fingers over her cheeks, just to check that she's really here, that she's OK. I feel the pound of her heartbeat against mine, the shake of her shoulders as she cries.

'I thought you were gone,' I whisper. 'I'm sorry. So sorry.'

Jasmine wraps her arm round my shoulder and I heave her up, wincing at her cry of pain. She grits her teeth, sucks the air in through them. I hate that she's hurting. Hate that this is all because of me.

We scramble up the slope, both crying and gasping. Every time I look up, it seems like we're no closer.

'Where is he? What's he doing?' Jasmine weeps.

I shake my head. I don't know. Please let him be gone. Please, just let this be over.

We're just steps away – so close – when Luke looms over the top, glaring down at us. Jasmine whimpers and we stumble back. My legs are aching so badly I don't know how much longer I can hold both of us up.

We try to move to the side, but Luke moves with us. He looks feverish and is rocking slightly on his heels, saying the same words over and over again: 'I never meant for her to die. I never meant for her to die. I never meant for her to die.'

'I'm not dead!' Jasmine says.

Luke's eyes narrow. I brace myself, waiting for his fist to thump into Jasmine's chest, plunging us to the bottom.

But he doesn't move. 'Not you,' he says. 'Hana.'

What? What's he saying? He's completely lost his mind! I have to get him to move, otherwise Jasmine and I are both dead. 'Luke, listen, I . . .'

'Luke?'

He flies round, his chest heaving.

There's someone else at the top of the ridge. 'What are you doing?' they ask. 'What's going on?'

Luke looks back at us. His face twists. He lets out this raw, bestial cry and makes a dash for the tree that the rope swing had been hanging from.

Jasmine and I crest the ridge, then collapse, our trembling limbs entangled and our hands firmly clasped.

Sadie is a couple of feet away, her face pale and almost unfamiliar with no make-up. She looks from Jasmine and me to Luke, who is trying to climb the tree. His movements are frantic and uncoordinated, his back stained with a dark patch of sweat. I can see how much he's shaking, even from here. He slips several times, but manages to reach the branch where the rope swing once hung. Luke fumbles in his pocket and draws something out. It glints in the sun.

My heart falls out of its ribcage. The penknife.

I'm on my feet in seconds. Sadie is two steps behind me,

talking into her phone. 'You need to get here now!' she says. 'He's going to hurt himself.'

At the base of the tree, I make a grab for the sturdy trunk, battling a wave of dizziness.

Luke has stretched his body along the branch so he's partially hanging over the drop. He stares at the blade, moving it back and forth as if he's mesmerised by it.

'It's all right, Luke,' Sadie says, in a voice that's so not Sadie: a voice that's gentle, calming. 'Why don't you come down and talk? Tell me what's going on.'

Luke ignores her and looks me dead in the eyes. 'I frayed the rope,' he says.

I shake my head. He can't have just said that, because it wasn't him. It was me. I frayed the rope.

'Did you know I'd asked Hana out, Megan? Did she tell you?'

'What?'

He repeats himself, louder, saying each word as if I'm deaf. 'I asked her out! Did you know?'

I shake my head.

'She turned me down. For Owen. So I sabotaged his stupid swing. I wanted to embarrass him. I never meant for anyone to die. And not Hana. It was never supposed to be Hana.'

It was Luke? He messed with the swing. It wasn't me. It wasn't my fault. But it's been my truth for so long, it must be right. The guilt has infested my body, turned my thoughts to venom, imprisoned my voice, weighed down my every step, but none of it was real. It can't be true. Please say it wasn't all for nothing. Don't tell me I didn't deserve to be punished, because I did. I know I did!

'It was me and Owen who moved the swing,' Sadie says, tears pooling in her eyes.

'But it was *me* who damaged the rope!' Luke spits, waving the blade.

He looks straight at me. 'I'm sorry.'

My breath stops. Sorry? Sorry doesn't even begin to cover it!

'I don't know how this happened … It was never supposed to get this far … God, what have I done? Oh, God, please …' Luke's speech unravels until he's just gibbering, crying, pleading. Sadie and I try to talk to him, but I don't think he can hear us any more. When Sadie starts to climb the tree, Luke snaps back to himself, shuffling further along the branch, which creaks and bends over the perilously steep decline.

Sadie backs away. Luke unwraps one arm from the branch, wobbles, almost falls, but catches himself. He raises a quivering hand to his wrist and places the blade against it.

'No!' Sadie and I both scream at the same time.

'Luke,' I gasp, 'please come down.'

'But it's my f-f-f-fault!' he cries, pressing the blade deeper.

'You couldn't have known that Sadie and Owen would move the swing,' I say quietly. 'Neither of us could. Just come down.'

There's the crackle of a radio behind us and we all turn, looking past Jasmine to two police officers, breathing deeply after the sprint up to the ridge.

'Stay away!' Luke shouts, brandishing his knife. 'I'll do it!'

The officer nearest to us – a freckled guy with a mop of ginger hair – stops and tells his colleague not to move.

I hold out my hand to Luke, even though there's no way I can reach him. My throat is clogged with all the words I want to say, but I have to get them out. 'I know you. This isn't you. This isn't the same guy who used to swap the pickled onion crisps in his lunch box for my KitKat, or the guy who spent half an hour chasing my gerbil around the living room when it escaped. You're still Luke.'

He stares at me for what seems like an age. Then he nods once. Luke's face crumples and his hands tense into claws as he starts to wail. The knife falls through his fingers and hurtles into the ridge.

Seconds later, the ginger-haired policeman is deftly climbing the tree, all the time talking to Luke, reassuring him.

I stagger back to Jasmine.

'What just happened?' she asks. 'What the hell just happened?'

As she starts to cry, I hold her, murmuring into her hair, telling her it's OK, it's over now, she's safe.

We don't move for a long time. We just sit on the grass, clutching each other, listening to the wail of sirens in the distance. The other police officer – a doughy, middle-aged woman – comes to check if we're all right. She says there's more help on the way, then she returns to Luke, who's sitting at the base of the tree, staring at nothing.

'How did he get you up here?' I ask Jasmine.

'I was so stupid!' she cries. 'I bumped into him on my way home. I was in a state – completely in shock – and he was so nice. Said he'd tell me everything, the whole story, if I came here with him. I didn't even think. I just got on the back of his bike. Such an idiot!'

'Shhhh. You weren't. It was my fault,' I whisper. 'I shouldn't have let you leave without explaining properly.'

We hear the brush of grass against Sadie's trainers as she approaches. She's trying not to meet our eyes, but she doesn't seem to know where else to look. Sadie wraps her arms around her waist. She looks so different today, in a pair of grey jogging bottoms and a black hoodie, her hair unstraightened and tied loosely in a ponytail.

Sadie sighs. 'Well, that was ... God, I don't even know what to say.'

I frown, wondering – for the first time – what she's doing here. She reads my expression and holds up a bunch of wilting flowers. 'You don't have the monopoly on guilt, Megan. If we hadn't moved the stupid thing ... Plus, I was the one who dared her to get on it. My so-called friends think I messed with the rope. Did you know that? They're actually scared of me!' She laughs without humour.

Jasmine and I just look at her.

Sadie glances at Luke. The police have handcuffed him, but wrapped him in a blanket, and they're both talking to him earnestly. 'I'm – er – sorry about Luke,' Sadie mutters.

'Thanks for ... Well, thanks for distracting him,' Jasmine says. 'I think ...' She blinks several times, as if she's only just imagined what might've happened if Sadie hadn't arrived. 'I think you might have saved us.'

Sadie kicks at a tuft of grass, picks a snapped flower head off the bunch, rolls it in her fingers, then lets it drop to the ground. 'God, this is so messed up.' She stares hard at the crushed flower. Her skin flares. 'Um, listen, Megan. I found this in my room the other day. I … well … I hadn't looked at it properly. How was I supposed to know who it was from? You should've just told me. Anyway. Sorry.'

She digs through her cavernous handbag, pulls out a creased envelope, chucks it down, mutters something about checking where the paramedics are, then leaves.

I stare at it. I can't pick it up. If I do, it might disintegrate, disappear.

'What is it?' Jasmine asks.

I swallow, manage to push each word out. 'It's Hana's last letter.'

CHAPTER THIRTY-TWO

A couple of days later, Jasmine and I are sitting beneath a beech tree. There's a stream close by and it tinkles in the background, relaxing and hypnotic. I pick a blade of grass and lift it to my nose, breathing in the heady, familiar smell.

Jasmine tilts her face up and her lips find mine. She kisses me tenderly, stroking my face as though she's making a map of it in her mind. I tangle my fingers through her glossy hair, breathing in the floral scent that wafts up from it.

We break apart, smiling, then link hands. We are silent. Still. Content.

I reach for my rucksack, unzip the front pocket and draw out Hana's letter. I take a deep breath. Let it out. I trace the groove where she scribbled my name.

'OK,' I say.

Jasmine gives my hand a squeeze. 'It's all right. Whatever it says, it's all right.'

My tongue sticks to the roof of my mouth. I try to swallow. I tear the envelope open. I'm so shaky I can barely pull out the letter.

'Will you read it to me?' Jasmine asks.

I nod, careful not to let my tears drip on the paper.

Hana's writing is scruffy, frenzied, and slants across the page at an angle, as though she wrote it in a rush. '*Dear Megan,*' I read in a wavering voice. '*I'm on my way to the ridge. I just wanted to stop and write you a quick note to say I'm sorry for being an arse about this whole thing. I hate fighting with you. I've missed you loads this week.*'

The tears are coming so fast I can barely see. But Jasmine's here, holding me. 'Read the rest,' she prompts. 'Finish it.'

I shake my head, but Jasmine points to the letter, insisting, so I continue, dragging the words out between sobs. '*Even if I do start hanging around with Sadie and Grace again, I promise – I swear, Megan – I'll never leave you behind. You're my best friend. You always will be. Nothing and no one will ever change that. Love, Hana.*'

The letter falls from my hand and flutters to the ground. I watch it, stunned. I'm drowning again, but this time, Jasmine's keeping me afloat. I clutch her, crying, and she doesn't let go until I'm done.

We stay for the rest of the afternoon. I lie with my head in Jasmine's lap. I think I maybe doze a little. I try to pick out the different birdcalls as they chatter in the trees above, remembering what Grandpa taught me. I imagine him cocking his head to one side as he listened, then pulling out his dog-eared bird book and asking me to point to those I recognised.

I catch a movement in the grass not far away. It's a bird: skinny and scraggly. I think its wing is injured. I nudge Jasmine and we both watch it try to fly. Every time it manages to lift a few centimetres, it falls back down again. I know how it feels.

I glance up at Jasmine. She's chewing her lip, watching the poor creature intently, willing it on. Then a smile breaks across her face and her eyes shine with delight. I look back. The bird has taken off and is flying higher and higher towards the sky.

The next day, I burst through our front door, clutching an envelope.

Mum's at the kitchen table, and instantly leaps up. 'Have you opened it?' she demands.

'Not yet.'

'Well, come on then. Quickly!'

I hold out the letter. 'You do it.'

The corners of her eyes crinkle. 'Really?'

'Yes, but now!'

Mum rips the envelope, then scans my results.

'Well?'

She grins. I think I can see the glisten of tears. 'Three As, six Bs, one C. You clever cow! I'm so bloody proud of you.'

Wow. I did well. Really well!

My smile falters. 'What do you think will happen to Luke's results?'

'I suppose his mum will take them to him.'

Luke's in some kind of secure unit now. Mum spoke to Sandra, who said it's early days, but he'll be getting really good psychiatric care. I just hope he's not too far gone to be helped.

Mum tilts my chin so I have to look at her. 'There's nothing you could've done, Megan. You're not taking responsibility for this.'

'No. I won't. I'm not.'

No more guilt.

There's an impatient knock on the door. I grin at Mum and rush to open it. Jasmine bounds in. 'What did you get? Tell me, tell me!' she squeals.

I laugh as she heads down the corridor, hobbling slightly on her bad ankle.

'Three As, six Bs, one C,' Mum calls from the kitchen. 'Think I've got a genius on my hands.'

'Megan, that's amazing!'

'What about you?' I ask.

'Two As, four Bs, a couple of Cs. I can't remember the rest! I just know it's enough to get me into Barcham Green,' Jasmine says as we join Mum in the kitchen. 'So, are you packed?'

'Pretty much.'

'Have you got sun cream?' Mum asks.

'Yes.'

'A hat?'

'Yes.'

'I can't wait!' Jasmine shrieks, clapping her hands together. 'I'm going to take you to all the best places, introduce you to loads of my old friends. We're going to stuff ourselves with amazing food. You'll have put on half a stone by the time I've finished with you, Megan. Oh, and I know the best bar to buy cocktails.' She glances at Mum. 'Non-alcoholic, of course.'

Mum rolls her eyes and smiles.

Jasmine follows me around the house as I finish packing, providing me with detailed descriptions of everything we're going to do, eat and drink in Cyprus. I can't believe I'm really going! My first holiday abroad.

We lug my suitcase down the stairs and leave it by the front door.

'Dad will be here in an hour,' Jasmine says. 'Is that everything?'

I reach into my bag and feel a familiar shape. 'I've just got to do one thing first.'

Jasmine squeezes my arm, plants a soft, sweet kiss on my lips, and heads off to find Mum.

I drag my bike from the utility room and head out the door.

Fifteen minutes later, I'm at the top of Stonylea Hill. I leave my bike at the side of the road and enter the forest, instantly feeling the effect of its quiet calmness. As I follow my own, personal trail, my fingers brush against spiky holly leaves, coarse twigs and spongy moss. I come across a couple of ponies whose shaggy manes flop around their faces. They stare at me for a moment, then continue foraging in the undergrowth.

When I reach the fallen oak, I kneel beside it, lean my forehead against the bark, and take a moment to breathe in the forest.

I pull a letter from my bag, read her name one last time, then place it in the hollow beneath the tree.

CHAPTER THIRTY-THREE

Dear Hana,

I hope you're happy, wherever you are. I'll always miss you.

Goodbye.

Megan xxx

ACKNOWLEDGEMENTS

I wish there were space on the cover to mention all the wonderful people who gave something to this book. First, my thanks to Mum and Dad, for filling my childhood with stories, for their support – emotional and financial – from the beginning; for all the writing courses, retreats, workshops, conferences, the degree . . . I'll stop now! Thank you.

My love and gratitude to my grandparents, particular thanks to Gran Sylvie, for telling me such beautiful tales about her and Grandpa Joe, and letting me share some of them here.

To my agent, Jodie Hodges, for her hard work, dedication and perseverance; for never losing faith.

Thank you to my editor, Kate Agar, for welcoming me so wonderfully to Little, Brown, for her incredible enthusiasm, for understanding the heart of Megan's story and helping me remain true to it, while pushing me to make it better.

Rather greedily, I have two writing groups. To everyone in WordWatchers: thank you for providing encouragement, criticism and cake in equal measures. I'm also grateful to the members of Swallows, particularly Nick Cook, for their honest feedback and their passion for *Unspeakable*.

I'm very lucky to count some talented editors among my friends. Thanks to Ali Pickford, who carefully teased out my plot holes, and Kersti Worsley, who is always so generous with her time, support and creativity.

I owe so much to Saras Grant and O'Connor and the Society of Children's Book Writers and Illustrators, who helped this undiscovered voice become discovered. Big love to the Undiscovered Voices 2010 gang.

To Charlie Evans, for her constant belief, and for telling me what I needed to hear. Also Katy Parks, for being such an inspiration. Thanks as well to Kerry Steed, for being honest about her early experiences, and for critiquing with such a professional and experienced eye.

To everyone who has offered expert knowledge to stop me from embarrassing myself, in particular Emily George and Jane McLoughlin. Any remaining mistakes are my own.

Finally, to my fiancé, Nick, who will be my husband by the time this is published. Thank you for always saying the right thing, for listening, sympathising, gently nagging. For tidying up around me, making sure I was fed, and for the many, many cups of tea. Where would I be without you?

Abbie Rushton grew up in a small village near Newmarket, Suffolk. She has a degree in English Literature with Creative Writing from the University of East Anglia, and is an editor at a leading educational publisher.

Whilst working as a part-time bookseller during her studies, Abbie rediscovered a love of children's and young adult books. In 2010, she was a winner of Undiscovered Voices, a writing competition run by the Society of Children's Book Writers and Illustrators.

Abbie lives near Newbury, Berkshire. She is a keen traveller and is never happier than when she is planning her next adventure.